© Patrick Forsyth 2021

All rights reserved

Without limiting the rights under copyright reserved above, no part of this publication may be
reproduced, stored in or introduced into a retrieval system, or transmitted, in any form or by any
means (electronic, mechanical, photocopying, recording or otherwise) without prior written
permission of the copyright owner

The right of Patrick Forsyth to be identified as author of this work has been asserted in accordance
with sections 77 and 78 of the Copyright, Designs and Patents Act, 1988

This book is a work of fiction. Names, characters, businesses, organisations, places, and events are
either the product of the author's imagination or are used fictionally. Any resemblance to actual
persons, living or dead, events or locales is entirely coincidental.

This Edition Published by Stanhope Books, Hertfordshire, UK 2022

www.stanhopebooks.com

Cover design and format by James Tiffin © 2021

ISBN-13: 978-1-909893-19-1

Dedication

In memory of Jack, my wonderful long term, long distance and holiday friend, sadly now very much missed.

God laughs when you steal from a thief.

Indian proverb.

Prologue

Something of a risk

Just six more paces to go. He moved one slow and careful step at a time, concerned that the floor in the house might creak. He was always very careful and was well aware that the stakes today might be higher than usual, even by his standards. He took a gentle step forward once more, paused, and focused on his listening, but there was no sound to be heard.

It had started with an overheard conversation in an East End pub. He had only heard a snatch of what was being said as two men were getting up to go, but he recognised the name of who they were speaking about: George Godwin. The man was a real, dyed in the wool, crook. He had dabbled in most things but was known to specialise in armed robbery of anything from jewellers and banks to the houses of the rich. He was known for being ruthless and for being a man never to cross; most people who knew of him gave him a wide berth. No one was thought to know him well, he was something of a loner, only his reputation and rumour, both untrustworthy, made him well known in criminal circles.

What was said in the pub was that it was rumoured that he had decided to retire. He had long had a villa in Portugal and was now thought to be set to move there permanently. That had prompted a thought: if the rumour of his move was true, then he would surely be taking some of his spoils with him; the situation seemed to indicate an opportunity. It took a bit of thinking through and there was something of a risk, and clearly a higher risk than he would like or was used to incurring. But the house where Godwin lived in a posh part of Chigwell was located without problem and a little research showed that it had recently started to display a 'For Sale' sign. The rumour did really look like it was true and the possibility of an opportunity remained. He checked, travelling to Chigwell and walking the area surrounding Godwin's expensive looking Victorian Mansion, which did indeed appear to be up for sale. In addition he noticed that there was no sign of Godwin's Aston Martin, habitually parked outside the house to impress. It seemed likely that he had driven to an airport.

It was a quiet neighbourhood, but he had a brief conversation with a neighbour, an elderly woman parked at the kerb and about to go into a house a few doors along, and learnt that she thought he had gone abroad, a few days at that villa of his she thought.

"Something," she said, "he seems to do quite often these days". If there was an opportunity it seemed to be a current one.

He took a further step across the study, a room the furnishings of which shouted money but which seemed at odds with the style of the Victorian house. As he swung his torch round he took in a glass topped desk, a bookshelf with only one book on it and a plethora of computer kit with a screen which seemed to be the size of the side of a bus. Now he was closer to his objective he could see that the opinion he had formed was right, the picture in front of him was not hung in the usual way but rather fastened to the wall and hinged on the left hand side, the classic disguise for a wall safe, though not a very effective one for anyone who knew safes. And he did know safes, he knew all about safes; if he had a speciality it was locks and safes, and as it was a practical speciality not an academic interest, there was very little he could not break into or open up. It was a skill that had served him well over the years and which he hoped would do so again tonight. He tugged on the shoulder strap of the bag slung round his neck, pushing it further onto his back as he took the final steps.

He swung the picture, a seascape he noted which could have been in the Algarve, aside and the matt black door of a safe was revealed. He held his breath for a moment and listened, but there was still no sound, the house did appear to be empty. Somewhere outside in the dark he heard a dog bark, the sound muffled by the distance. He adjusted his glasses and went to work.

About forty minutes later, a few minutes longer than he had anticipated, he relocked the safe and again slung his bag around his neck and onto his back as he retraced his steps out from the study and through into the entrance hall. Stairs curved up to his left, but mindful of the risk he was taking he rejected any idea of extending his search in that direction and resolved to leave the house without any further delay. Now convinced beyond all doubt that the house was indeed empty, and having dealt with the alarm on his way in, he saw no reason not just to leave by the front door and he walked at a measured pace across the hall towards it. As he reached for the handle without any warning the door flew open towards him letting light flood in from a lamp in the porch and revealing the tall figure of George Godwin, arrived home off a flight from Porto, and holding a smart wheeled suitcase in one hand raised to lift it up and over the front step. The shock he felt was palpable, he jerked back and his shoulder bag sagged to one side and nearly slipped off. In just a second or two as he struggled to regain his equilibrium he saw that Godwin had reached into his coat pocket and was holding a small stub-nosed automatic pistol. He well knew that he was facing a man guaranteed to take very great offense at an unexpected intruder in his house at two in the morning. The look on Godwin's face confirmed the fact beyond all doubt. Fear gripped him and his mind raced.

Two doors down the road in the quiet and sleeping neighbourhood an elderly lady was returning to her bed having been roused by her alarm to give her sick cat the next due dose of medicine. She barely noticed the slight sound that in fact came from next door but one, and certainly did not ponder what it was when, only a few minutes after Godwin had arrived home and discovered an intruder, a single gunshot had rung out in his hall.

Chapter One

This might be it

If she had to do this for one more hour she felt she would go and jump off the nearest bridge. Luckily she didn't have to, it was her last day. It was not really a matter of luck, she had not actually been fired but her trial period had not, she had been told in no uncertain terms, been extended. She would not have minded if she never saw another supermarket in her entire life. She had rarely ever been out front meeting customers, that might have been more tolerable, she would have quite liked that, but rather she had spent most of her days buried in the back premises, a nether world of cardboard and noise where the most exciting thing she had to do was flattening cardboard boxes ready for disposal. She saw stuff coming in and she saw what it had been packed in when it arrived going out.

She had hated it all so much that she had even contemplated a final act of sabotage as she left. She thought that if she used a long piece of string arranged as a tripwire and linked from display to display she could probably get a dozen or more towers of product to topple like dominoes once it was triggered by someone's unwary foot. That would be something to make her misery-guts supervisor weep, but it was fantasy, of course, and in the end she decided not to play any such trick. Truth be told her career prospects were not the best and she did not want repercussions that might further blight her future. She tied up her last bundle of cardboard as her shift ended, checked her watch and walked out. She did not look back, though she thought back: this was her second job departure within three weeks. At her last place, she had a waitressing job in a large local bistro, she had fallen out with the manager when she had pointed out that he was not passing on the majority of the tips received to his staff. He had given her a tip: find another job. Things had to change.

She walked towards Chapel Market, a bustling street packed with stalls and small shops situated off the end of Essex Road in London's Islington, she weaved her way through the crowds of people, the sound of flapping canvas from the stalls and the shouts of stall-holders intent on encouraging custom ringing in her ears. It was a place of constant hubbub. Half way along the street she stepped into a doorway to try to minimise the noise and phone her mother.

"Hi Mum, where are you?" She had arranged to meet her mother and help with some shopping, but she knew it would end in more nagging about her getting what her mother always called 'proper work'.

"Where do you think I am, Tracy? Waiting for you on the corner where we planned, that's where. Where are you?"

"Sorry Mum, I'm in the market, I saw a sign this morning asking for an apprentice – at the locksmith's – you know, a shop up the far end. I'm going to go and talk to them, okay?" She thought it politic not to remind her mother that it had been her last day at the supermarket and that she was now jobless... again.

"Yeah, alright, you really must do something. I suppose I'll manage. See you later." Her mother ended the call.

Tracy realised that the only excuse for not helping with the shopping that her mother would accept was something linked to getting a new job. She knew her mother had a point; what she thought of as nagging, was actually only sensible, and she had been thinking about what she said more and more in recent weeks. She had come to admit that she was in a deep rut; it was depressing and she had to get out of it somehow. Since she saw the sign in the morning she had not stopped thinking about it. It was a small shop, and as she had hated being a minion amongst minions at the supermarket so much that appealed, and it involved a real trade. Having had no real ideas what to do since she left school she had begun to find that the thought of that was interesting. It was clear work at the locksmiths involved real face to face contact, helping people, and it was not just cutting keys, they dealt with safes and security too. She reckoned she could do worse and as far as she knew the job did not involve cardboard.

As she got close to the shop she could see that the sign was still in the window, no explanation, just 'Apprentice wanted'. Another sign on the door indicated that the shop was closed: it actually read: *Locked up (Sorry: that means closed)*. As she walked closer a man was moving away from the door apparently having locked up for the day. She hurried forward, motivated as much as anything by not wanting to return home and tell her mother that there was nothing to report.

"Hang on, please hang on."

Hearing her shout, the man turned towards her. He was about sixty she reckoned, not too tall and looked neat and tidy in a sports jacket and tie. How many people wear a tie to man a small shop she thought? He had a kindly face and was wearing horned rim glasses that appeared to be a size too large for him.

"What is it, where's the fire?" He smiled as he saw her hastening towards him, seeing a good-looking young woman dressed in ripped jeans and a stained sweatshirt and with her blond hair tied back in a ponytail.

"Can I have a word about your sign – the apprentice thing that is?"

"Well, I've just locked up. But… you interested?"

She felt her chances of speaking with him were already slipping away, but continued: "Yes, I am, well I think I am."

There was what seemed like a long pause while he looked her up and down, then saying: "What's your name then?"

"Tracy, Tracy Hines." She paused, not sure what else to say, then noticed the way he was scrutinising her and added: "Sorry, I'm not looking very smart, I've had an overall on over all this through the day."

"Well not-very-smart Tracy Hines, do you fancy a cuppa, we could go to the café and chat for a few minutes?"

"Yes, yes, that's good. Thank you. Lead on." He turned and walked away and she followed staying close behind, the market was noisy and she did not attempt any more conversation as they walked, twisting and turning through people to avoid a collision. Once sitting in a small café just round the corner he asked her what she wanted to drink and went to the counter to order. Tracy looked around her: it was not one of the ubiquitous chain outlets, rather an independent establishment and its rough and ready appearance seemed very much part of the market. A coffee machine spluttered at one end of the counter and around her the place was about half full of people of all ages and types. He soon returned with two coffees one of which he put in front of her, she thanked him and took a sip as she waited for him to ask a question.

"So, what makes you think you want to be a locksmith? I'm not after someone just to serve customers at the counter you know, I want someone to learn the trade, to help with everything." The way he said it made it sound at once more interesting, it was not just a shop, not just customer service; it was – a trade. She took a big breath.

"Mr Holmes, is that right?" She knew what it said on the shop front: Holmes & Son.

"Yes, but call me Marty."

"Okay, thanks, and thanks for talking to me and for the coffee. I'm... I'm... well." She paused trying to think what to say and found little to recommend herself. She took a deep breath. "Okay, let me be honest with you, I've few qualifications, I have just finished a trial period in the worst supermarket job in the world, I never want to recycle cardboard boxes again as long as I live, but I need a job and... the thing is I have to find something interesting, or I shall die of boredom."

She paused, uncertain how to go on.

"What we do is quite technical in its way, you know it's..." She found herself interrupting.

"Yes, yes, but it sounds interesting, and I want to learn. I didn't do well at school but I'm not stupid, actually I think I'm quite bright, I just got distracted from the exam thing at school, you know. And I can smarten up a bit." Saying this seemed to embarrass her and she looked away.

"Okay, tell me a little about yourself, apart from the exams."

Tracy gave him a rapid overview: saying that she lived at home with her mother in flats on the city side of Islington down by the canal; she could walk to the shop in a few minutes. Her father had disappeared when she was eleven (she was not quite twenty one), she had not done well at school, which she had hated, and having had a number of unsatisfactory jobs she had now realised – not before time she admitted - that what she really needed was not just a job but a chance to learn something useful, something that would fit her for a role she would find interesting.

"It was exams that were my downfall, I reckon I'm bright enough... I've said that haven't I? Sorry. I could read a bit before I even started school and I play the guitar a little, though sorry again... that's hardly relevant, is it? I'm not doing too well at this, am I? But I *am* interested, I so want to have a job I like."

Marty did not answer for a moment, he lifted his mug and took a measured sip and lowered it back down with what seemed to be great precision. Finally, he replied:

"I could never play a musical instrument, though I guess your doing so means that you are manually dextrous as well as musical and you need that for this job, the dextrous bit that is, not the music. You're not going to run off and join a band, are you?"

"No, I'm not that good and you wouldn't want to hear me sing." She grinned, then had another thought:

"Also, I reckon I am pretty dextrous, I've always been the one to do the DIY at home and, now I think, about it, I quite like doing it. I haven't had a shelf fall down yet."

"Well, I have to say that I imagined anyone I took on would be a little older and rather better turned out than you, a man, I assumed – forgive me that, though now I think of it I'm not sure why - and have a technical qualification of some sort... and an employment record that indicated some small degree of reliability." He paused again, and Tracy felt things did not sound very good at all. She said nothing.

"But you know what, I think we might make it work, I like that you have been honest about yourself and you seem genuinely ready for a challenge and, while I'm prejudiced, I very much reckon this is an interesting job. I'm not getting any younger so I want someone to learn the business and help with everything, as I said it's not just sitting behind the counter cutting keys and selling padlocks. Let me give you some details." He described the little shop as having been his father's, that he had only ever had an assistant to help serve at the counter before, but now wanted someone to get involved and help across the board. He explained that much of the work was outside – everything from getting people into a house for which they had lost the keys or changing locks after a burglary to work on safes – and set out the money and terms he had in mind. He also said that he would give her an advance, a week's money at the end of the first week before going onto a monthly basis.

"How does that sound? If I give you a chance, once we know if the work suits you and that you have an ability for it we can review things. My dad taught me and I think I'll enjoy teaching someone else. When can you start?"

"All sounds good. Tomorrow?"

"No, better make it Monday, give me chance to get organised. Write your name and address down, and a phone number, and I'll write you a confirmation, we should have some formality about it all, but I'll give you the letter when you come in on Monday, okay?"

"Very okay, thanks for giving me a chance Mr… Marty. See you Monday then, nine o'clock."

"On the dot; that's rule one." He grinned and found a scrap of paper for her to write her contact details on before they went their separate ways. When she got home Tracy had great pleasure in telling her mother that she had got what she described as a "proper job." At his home Marty told his wife that he had finally had a single application for the post at the shop and that luckily enough it was someone who suited well and who he was in the process of taking on. He said little about her to his wife at this stage, he hoped he was right about Tracy, she hardly appeared ideal, he was going with his gut and just reckoned there was something about her; time would tell.

On Monday morning Tracy was outside the shop door at 8.50. First impressions last she knew and punctuality spoke volumes and was something Marty seemed to value.

"Morning you!" A cheerful voice at her elbow startled her. Marty. He went on: "Right on time, I see, good start, let's get my little emporium opened up shall we?" He worked the keys as Tracy mumbled a good morning and, feeling a little apprehensive, then remained silent as they went inside.

Fifteen minutes later she was sitting on a stool behind the counter with a mug of coffee in front of her and feeling better already. Marty welcomed her with enthusiasm, noting to himself that the jeans she wore were no longer torn and that she looked quite smart, as he explained that he had got her what would be 'your stool' and that from now on she would deal with three kinds of thing.

"It's like this see, first there's things you can do immediately such as selling an item like a padlock off the shelf, you said you can work a till having worked in bars so that's easy. Next there's things you'll pick up pretty quickly like cutting keys, most get the hang of that machine in a day or two - it's really very straightforward. And don't worry, I'll show you. Then thirdly there is more complicated stuff, safes and so on. I'll let you come out with me and watch that sort of thing to start with, there'll be a good bit of learning and practice involved in that area, but if you want to do it all there is no reason why you can't."

It was clear that Marty took the term apprentice seriously, as the morning went on he hardly stopped talking, Tracy watched him cutting keys, as he responded to what was a common customer request, she stood close so that she could see properly and found herself getting sprayed with the metallic dust that flew up as he worked. A few hours in she realised just how different from anything else she had done this was. Customers were pleasant, in true small shop style, they chatted a bit and they wanted help and advice not just directions to what aisle something was in that was all she had ever heard said in the supermarket.

Come lunchtime, Marty declared a break was due and sent her out and to get them a sandwich each and a coffee. He had explained earlier that there would be "a few dogsbody jobs along the way" and this was evidently one of them. A little later Marty came out from the rear stockroom and office at the back of the shop holding two printed sheets.

"Outside jobs now" he said. "Some poor soul is sitting on the pavement locked out of his house and then there's a safe that needs opening – let's get you seeing some of the range of stuff we do. You up for that?"

"Yes, of course, it's…" she paused. "…I do find it fascinating." They set off and Tracy found that there was a shop van kept in a lock up not far away. The locked out man proved to be at a smart house in Arlington Square, situated not far from the block of flats where Tracy lived.

"Parking's a problem in this job," said Marty as they pulled up "but with this sort of thing we can just stop at the kerb and keep an eye on the van from inside, well outside in this case, it's a doorstep job."

"Oh, great, thanks so much for coming." A man dressed in a smart business suit came down a step or two from the house to greet them. He pointed: "The key's down that drain and my wife is out of town, you are an absolute godsend." There followed something of an inquisition as Marty first satisfied himself that the guy was actually the owner of the house. Then he set to, explaining to Tracy as he went along what he was doing.

"Just watch for the moment, we'll have you doing this sort of thing on your own soon enough." Job done and a relieved owner back inside his house they went on to tackle a safe. This was certainly more complicated and Tracy watched in awe as Marty worked. Like many a skilled tradesman he made what he did look effortless, though it still took a little while to gain entry. She watched as the door clicked open and marvelled.

Back in the shop the day continued with what Marty described as "routine", nevertheless as the end of the day arrived Tracy found she had found it all interesting.

"Time to lock up, day one over. What do you think?" Asked Marty.

"It's been great, thank you, I know you are taking a chance with me, but if today is anything to go by it's going to be great. Sorry, I must stop saying great. I mean I found it a good experience and look forward to more, and that's something I never said in the supermarket."

"Take this home." As they prepared to close up Marty put a lock attached to a block of wood down on the counter. "Only if you want, of course, I'll show you tomorrow how to go about opening it so soon you will know enough to practice at home - and practice makes perfect as they say. You might even get hooked on it, like a puzzle. Tell you what, I'll give you a tenner if you can open that up unaided within a month." Tracy found she did want to take it, she said nothing but nodded her head to indicate her agreement, they found a bag and she made to leave the shop.

"Off you go then, see you tomorrow." Marty gave her a wave as she gathered up her bag and set off for home. As Tracy took the lock and walked away through the market she had something of a spring in her step, she really thought that at last this might be it. It was, of course, early days but she already reckoned she was going to be a locksmith.

Chapter Two

An ideal little expedition

A few nights before taking on his somewhat unlikely apprentice, Marty had been out late.

There was a satisfying click and Marty pulled his hands back an inch as he removed the two slim stainless-steel probes from the door lock. He was in. He slipped the probes back into a well-worn leather case that he had inherited from his father years ago. As he stood still listening outside the door at the back of the house, he dwelt for a moment on how lax so many people tended to be about their home security. The lock in front of him was doubtless regarded by its owner as adequate, probably more than adequate, yet it had taken Marty only two or three minutes to hear the sound of that satisfying click and gain access to the house. He had reckoned to have to deal with an alarm first, but when he tapped the yellow box on the side of the house with a long cane he had found in the garden it made a hollow sound. It was obvious that it was an empty box: he knew this to be common, people went for what they thought was a visible deterrent and saved the money on purchasing an actual system. False economy, thought Marty, as he opened the door a crack and, ever careful, paused for a moment focusing on listening alone, then swung it open wide, entered the house and closed the door behind him without making a sound.

He knew the family whose house it was to be in Italy where they were on holiday. He should have no problem tonight and set about searching for a safe. He continued to keep his ears tuned for any sound though; he was a careful man, always had been, a trait he had inherited as he followed in his father's footsteps. He had been doing this all his life and had not been caught once. It was a record he very much intended should continue. As a locksmith by trade, running his small shop just as his late father - who had, as they say, taught him all he knew - had done, he had learnt not just about the business and the skills that involved but also about his secondary trade. Along with his careful nature he had inherited the shop and all the tools of that trade from his father, though there were some items that were not recorded anywhere for prying eyes to notice and that went rather beyond those of a routine locksmith business.

Marty was very selective; he did not burgle just anyone, and he did not do it every five minutes. He was careful, yes, but the business – he liked to think of it in that way – inevitably also involved some luck. The unexpected could surely happen and might then create circumstances that could lead to his apprehension. So he had a routine, he never did too many jobs, in fact only a few each year, just enough to raise the income he got from his shop so that he and his wife could enjoy nice holidays and he could indulge his great love of classic cars. Sometimes his criminal activities occurred less often, especially if the last job produced a good sum, and each one had to be just right. Low risk was an absolute priority. Tonight, was a case in point.

His notice had first been drawn to Terence Fowler as a name in a news item in the newspaper. He was what the story referred to as an entrepreneur, which actually meant he ran a number of businesses and apparently did so with scant regard for anything but money: the story concerned one such business – a printers – closed down virtually overnight with no concern for the welfare of the employees and, the paper suggested, for no better reason than the company made little money and Fowler could not be bothered with it any more. He had put the site up for sale for development just days after the doors closed for the last time, a move that looked like making him a great deal of money. Googling him had shown nothing good being said about him; he was just the sort of person Marty wanted to locate as he liked to think that, although what he did was undeniably criminal, he did not hurt anyone, well not anyone that mattered. Marty was realistic, he knew he was not performing a public service, but he had always had a code, something else inherited from his father, and those he robbed had to fit in with that private code. It was an absolute principle and one that helped him sleep easy.

Without much difficulty some further research soon showed where Fisher lived and a careful appraisal on visiting the house suggested that getting in would present little problem. He would never go into a house blind, but was also careful to do any physical checking out in a way that minimised the chances of his being seen in, or linked to, the area. On this occasion he had visited the house in the guise of delivering circulars – he kept some that arrived at his own home addressed just to 'The Occupier' and needed only one to put through the door and another to show anyone who might enquire what he was doing. He had walked up the drive and approached the front door. Sometimes, as on this occasion, luck was in his favour. The Fowlers had their milk delivered and on the doorstep was not only a couple of empty bottles but also a note poked out of one of them. Marty had gone away with a detailed description of just when Fowler wanted delivery paused as he was going on holiday. It had at that moment become confirmed as what he described to his wife Mary as 'an ideal little expedition'.

His wife knew what he got up to, she knew about it years back even before they got married, but she also knew of his philosophy regarding his 'expeditions' and approved of that situation too, her decisions linked to the lifestyle it gave them and the fact that Marty had never been caught. Over the years she got to take the situation for granted, he never gave her any details of what he got up to on the day, never said more than "I'll be on a little expedition tonight, love", and she found she dwelt on his clandestine activities and the potential jeopardy they inevitably presented less and less over the years. What he was doing, after all, was something that might be regarded as a family tradition.

Having gained access to Fowler's house Marty set about finding what he regarded as the inevitable safe. It was a sizeable house and he expected the kind of man Fowler was to have a study and, if so, that is likely where any safe would be. He went from the utility room into which he had entered from the back of the house, on into the kitchen and then to the spacious entry hall, there he soon found the study, the door stood open and his torch alighted on a large desk that acted as a sign post. All this Marty did by the light of a tiny pencil torch, which produced the light he needed but was insufficient to chance an inappropriate light being seen from outside the house. The safe confirmed the opinion he had formed of Fowler from his assessment of the alarm; his security was rudimentary. Occasionally Marty was faced with something that was a real challenge, indeed sometimes his commercial work gave him just that, in which case he could test his expertise with no fear of being arrested. Here there was no great challenge. The safe was in open view, secured to a shelf with screws inside itself, however the shelf was not solid wood but chipboard and anyone could have prised it free with a small crowbar and carried it away.

Marty did not favour brute force, and anyway taking the safe would extend the risk he was taking unnecessarily; he would have to dispose of it somewhere after opening it and that was one more thing that might expose him; an unnecessary thing in his view A few minutes of careful work and the safe door swung open. He had been right, this was owned by the kind of man whose financial affairs revolved largely around cash. There must have been twenty or thirty thousand pounds neatly bundled and only needing lifting out and transferring to his trusty shoulder bag. He did not pause to count it, even roughly - that could be done later.

He took a moment to look through the rest of the safe's contents. There were a fair number of documents; whatever they were Marty was not interested, he always kept things simple; he reckoned that the only result of complications was to produce surprises. There was a Rolex watch, presumably left at home as it was unsuitable for a beach holiday. Very nice, but although he might have been able to get a thousand pounds for it, Marty ignored it. Disposing of it would expose him too much and he had done well, there was plenty of cash. So, enough. He closed the safe, ears cocked for any sound, and retracing his steps he slipped out of the house and made his way back to his car, parked as usual a little way from the house. Things had gone just the way he wanted; "no problem, text book" he muttered to himself as he started the engine.

The money was secured away on his way back and he was parked up, home and creeping into bed by 2.00 a.m. His wife stirred slightly as he slipped between the sheets but did not wake. He did not set an alarm, he would open the shop tomorrow a little later than usual, not least so that he could take time to assure Mary that his expedition had been without any negative incident. For a while he had been thinking of getting some proper assistance in the shop, indeed he had a notice displayed in the window advertising the position. He closed his eyes and was asleep in moments.

Chapter Three

Progressing very nicely

Tracy had not only worked hard since starting at Holmes & Son, she had enjoyed it and had already learnt a great deal; she had been delighted to find that the work suited her well. She was beginning to think that Marty approved, but she had not noticed the exact date and was surprised when one morning Marty announced that the three month trial period that featured in her appointment was up.

"The time seems to have gone by quickly, I hope it has for you too… are you happy to have reached this landmark?" he asked.

"Well, that rather depends on whether you intend to keep me on now 'the landmark', as you call it, has passed."

"Yes, of course I do, you've done well, better than I dared to hope if I'm honest. But you know that and you may remember too that a small increase in your rate of pay is due now." Tracy gave a little bow, making light of it, but was secretly very pleased.

"Thank you, kind sir," she said. Marty smiled, he too was pleased. She really had done well and it was a great satisfaction to him that he had picked her, given her a chance and that his training had all been going well. Tracy was a fast learner and he did not often have to tell her anything twice. The morning passed in a routine way until Marty offered an invitation.

"Come on you, shut the shop for a while, we have to meet Mary. Lunch at the pub today by way of celebration, okay?" Tracy thanked him, she turned the sign and locked the door as they went and at twelve noon they were all sitting in the pub.

"I'll go to the bar, what do you want to drink, you two? Food too, proper food if you will, we can't celebrate with only a sandwich," said Marty. They scanned the menus, made their choices and he hurried off leaving Tracy and Mary together.

"I don't know what he's said to you," Mary said, "probably not enough knowing Marty, but he's really chuffed that you're doing so well. 'Progressing very nicely,' he said and from Marty that is high praise indeed. I hope you're enjoying the work, that's important too."

"I certainly am, I've never had a good job before, well you know, and this is so different. It's interesting and, you know what, I do reckon it suits me. I like it and I'm proving to be pretty good at it too, I think."

"Well, I'm pleased too, I don't hesitate so much now if I want Marty to take a long weekend off say, knowing you are beginning to cope so well. It's good all round." At that moment Marty appeared back with their drinks and told them food would be delivered shortly. They chatted for a while without talking any shop and Mary asked whether Tracy was still living at home with her mother. She said she was but also that it was not ideal, she really wanted her own space.

"But it's difficult round here, you know, expensive, and I would not want to be too far away, I can walk to the shop and I know the area, I've friends here." Mary sympathised, saying that they were lucky to have inherited their house from Marty's father, his mother having died earlier.

"Well, I know it's difficult but one day maybe... don't give up on the idea yet, eh."

The food Marty had ordered then appeared and they enjoyed a convivial lunch together. Marty reviewed something of what Tracy had learnt and what he had planned for her next. Tracy smiled to herself: this was so different from anything she had done before and she was really enjoying it. Her mother's attitude had changed too over the time she had worked with Marty. She no longer nagged about her needing to get a 'proper job', in fact she was interested in what Tracy was up to and how it was all going. It made for a much better atmosphere, even so Tracy still wanted to get a place of her own. At one point Mary forced them to change the subject.

"Too much shop Marty," she said, "sometimes you don't let Tracy get a word in."

There followed what would be a significant lesson for Tracy, as they avoided shop business, she asked Marty about his hobby and specifically about how work was going on his current car project. As she spoke she could see Mary shaking her head, but it was too late, Marty not only answered, he answered at length, only stopping when Mary interrupted him.

"This is supposed to be a celebration Marty, the poor girl is busy learning your trade, she doesn't want a lecture on motor renovation as well."

Chapter Four

Not his only concern

Some nine months later...

Things were progressing well for Marty, his appointment of an apprentice had worked out far better than he had dared to hope. On her first day Marty had let Tracy take home a lock 'for practice', within a fortnight she had brought it back and opened it for him in a matter of minutes, explaining that she got hooked on it and had spent some time on it every evening. He handed over the due tenner and congratulated her. His occasional 'little expeditions' had continued to be successful too. He had been out late the previous evening.

When Marty had woken in the morning the light was bright at the window and he was alone in bed. A quick glance at the clock by his bed showed that it had just gone 8.30 a.m. He was usually up at 7.00 but now he lay for a moment thinking about the events of his late night. There had been no hitches and he felt secure in his belief that all had gone well. He had made a good haul and the money he had 'released' was hidden away far from prying eyes. There was thus no need for a further expedition for a while, but even as he showered and shaved he dwelt on what he felt was becoming a good expedition idea for the future, something that was, however, time sensitive. If he was going to do it then it would have to be done in the near future. He got up and got himself ready for the day.

"Morning, love, how are you – how did it go last night?" Downstairs Mary greeted him from in front of the cooker, adding "I heard you on the move, so I'm doing you a fry up as you're not rushing this morning."

"Great, thanks, all well, but you know the form, the less you know about last night the better, eh." He chuckled and his wife said nothing in reply, changing the subject and asking about the shop. Their routine in such matters was well established.

"Tracy be okay opening up this morning?" The toaster popped up as she spoke and she laid a plate of bacon and eggs in front of him and turned to organise the toast onto a side plate.

"Yes, indeed, a real find that one, she's still doing really well. She's a natural. We had a lost key call out a couple of days ago, a guy running a jewellers who had lost the key to his safe – dropped it into the loo would you believe just as he flushed. Anyway it was beyond what she had ever done to date, I let her have first go at getting it open and was ready to give a bit of advice along the way, but, you know what? She had no problem. Textbook stuff, fast too, I'll have to watch myself I reckon, she has a fair old range these days."

"That's good, you needed someone reliable to work with, gives you more flexibility, you're not getting any younger you know." She smiled at him, they both knew it would be his 60th birthday in a few weeks' time. She continued: "After last night's expedition maybe we could have a weekend away at the coast, if you think that Tracy can cope on a Saturday. What do you think?"

"Good idea, no reason why not, Southend perhaps or we could go up into Suffolk, Southwold's nice. Let's talk about it this evening, I should get to the shop before too long. Don't want to be too late." He washed his breakfast down with a last swig of tea, gave Mary a kiss on the cheek and headed off to work leaving her with a cheery "See you later, love" ringing in her ears.

Marty's walk to work was an easy one. The shop was not far away, they lived in his parent's old house, a terrace north of the Essex Road in London's Islington; it was a location that allowed him to walk to work. Holmes & Son, the name had never been changed despite it being many years since Marty had worked there with his late father, occupied a small shop in nearby Chapel Market. The window displayed a variety of padlocks and other security paraphernalia, and was covered with a sliding security screen rather like the doors on old fashioned lifts, this bore a sign about the availability and installation of such things. A larger sign said "Keys cut". The shop had a look of being decidedly old fashioned but made its long establishment and specialist nature clear and had always done good business in the busy market.

The morning after Marty's late-night Tracy was there just before 9.00 a.m. and had the "Open" sign displayed right on time. She looked the part these days, long gone were the jeans replete with open wounds, she now always wore a man's tan leather waistcoat over a white shirt and had a badge with her name on it pinned to that. Her hair was always in a neat ponytail during working hours, it was a look she thought indicated a professional tradesperson. Much to her surprise she was taking pride in being just that. Almost before she could get behind the counter a first customer arrived, an elderly woman pushing a shopping trolley displaying vegetables, lying on top of various packages, which Tracy reckoned had been bought from the market stall almost immediately outside the shop.

"Can you do me a duplicate of this?" She waggled a key in front of Tracy as she spoke. Tracy took it in at a glance and answered with certainty. "Sure, it'll only take a few minutes, take a seat." The woman handed over the key with a polite "thank you" and sat down in the single chair next to the counter. Tracy had long had no problem with the key cutting machine and soon a buzzing sound filled the shop as she got to work. The job was soon done and, while doing it, Tracy learnt that the key was for the woman's daughter.

"She has a spare in case something happens to me, I'm not getting any younger you know, and last time she visited her youngster dropped the spare key down a drain at the kerb."

"Well, all done," said Tracy, "there you go, that'll be £5.50 please." Money was exchanged, thanks given and she shut the till drawer as the woman went on her way.

Tracy enjoyed the job. She reckoned she was lucky, given her lack of success at school, she had certainly not done well enough to go to university, and an apprenticeship, even such an informal one as she now had, was proving a good option, albeit one that had taken her a while to get in her sights. She was by no means unintelligent, it was more that "school had not suited her" as she put it. It had not helped that she had got on the wrong side of many of the teachers, though she admitted that had been mostly her fault. One exploit stood out: she had organised a group of mates to bodily lift one teacher's tiny Fiat 500, bouncing it sideways and wedging it tight nose to tail between two trees. Somehow she was the only one identified afterwards and it was no surprise that the teacher was not amused to say the very least. She was on detention for a long while. Now, with skilled tuition from Marty, she had proved a fast learner and was becoming seriously accomplished at her new trade. It was just her and Marty in the shop, there was nothing he did not know about the business and he was patient, he valued having an assistant and had been taking time and trouble to help her learn. On one job the other day she had even succeeded in opening a pretty complicated safe and reckoned she had it open in rather less time than Marty had been expecting. This had earned her a convincing sounding "Well done". But she reckoned Marty's face had told her more, he was surprised, proud and, while taking some of the credit himself for facilitating her growing expertise, he had, she reckoned, begun to rate her quite highly. Despite the difference in their ages, Tracy was only twenty-one, she got on well with him.

She could really see this becoming her career, she had done enough to know that she had something of a flair for it, and it was work in which she could in due course perhaps have her own business. In the meantime Marty's shop was providing something of a template. Besides there was something else.

Keen to learn she watched all that Marty did with care and gradually she had become to suspect that the shop was not his only concern; it seemed to her that something else was going on. It was only occasional little things, but they added up. For instance, sometimes packages would arrive that were not opened in her presence, but tucked away in what seemed to her a secretive fashion. More often he would ask her to open any parcels and to put whatever it was away in its designated place in the small room behind the counter, essentially a stockroom, but where there was also a desk. Here Marty attended to the paperwork the business involved, jobs that needed invoicing, suppliers' bills that needed paying and so on; he was briefing her on this aspect of what had to be done too. Sometimes Marty would spend an undue time at his desk and, if she came into the room, a folder would be shut in haste seemingly to prevent her seeing whatever he was looking at. Tracy reckoned it all added up. Then there were his occasional late mornings, like today. He always explained it away as being to make up for a late night, but there was never a very convincing explanation for why that had occurred. If it was something matter of fact, taking his wife to the cinema, theatre or out for a meal, then he would surely say so.

Given his particular skills Tracy began to think he was out breaking into a bank or some such. It was just a fancy, of course, and she wasn't to know that her imaginings were much more large scale than the truth of the matter, but she reckoned something like that fitted the facts. Besides she rather liked the idea of her boss being some kind of rogue. She resolved to probe more when he came in later. Meantime she had a request for a quotation to reply to: another lost key by the sound of it, albeit without any real urgency for the solution on this occasion.

As she sat at the computer and typed up the quotation, she kept an eye on the shop entrance through the open stockroom door and saw Marty arrive.

"Morning Tracy. Sorry, I'm late," he said, "you been coping alright?"

"Hi. Yes, all fine here, I'm just typing up a quotation, do you want to check it?"

"No need to read it, just give me a rough idea and tell me what cost you put in," Marty said. She gave him the details and he confirmed his agreement at once.

"That's fine, thanks." Marty thought on the fact that this girl really was a find, he resolved to give some more thought to her future and how he could bind her to the business.

"So, what were you up to last night then, some nefarious business I should know about?" Tracy waited eager to see what such a direct approach would produce, but Marty brushed it off.

"Oh, nothing much, just something with friends. Went on a bit." Tracy said no more but found that she was detecting a tangible bit of evasion in his tone and her suspicions deepened. Marty failed to read between the lines and spot her wonderings and continued to think that his secret remained just that. He led the way now, making a suggestion.

"Okay we must get on, we've another safe to tackle today, do you want to come? It's not far away and we can close the shop for a little while." Tracy jumped at the opportunity just as Marty expected. He was very pleased with her progress and, with the anniversary of her spending a year working for Holmes & Son almost upon them, he had been thinking about not only how to mark the occasion but also how to secure a firm future for her and lower the likelihood of her wanting to move on. He had made some decisions and written her a note that he planned to hand over to her on the actual date of her one year's service which was in just a few days' time.

After locking up they set off down the road in the direction of King's Cross, heading towards Marty's double garage, the lockup went back to the days when his father ran the business. In this he kept the small van with the business details emblazoned along the sides that they used to get to this sort of job. It also housed whatever classic car he was working on currently; there was always one. As Marty unlocked the garage doors and went to get into the van Tracy called out.

"I'll do the doors." She stood back as he reversed out, locked up after him and then got into the passenger seat. Marty pulled away and drove out of the cul-de-sac.

"What are you working on in there at the moment?" Asked Tracy thinking of the humped shape of an old saloon car she had seen inside the garage. She well knew it was a risky question, such things were Marty's greatest passion, and she was unlikely to get a short answer.

"It's a Jowett Javelin," he said, stating a name that meant nothing to her, "quite the thing in the fifties that was. This one was in a poor old state when I got her I can tell you, but I have just got her running in the last month or so. It's a great car. Mind you, I'll probably sell it on in due course, once I find another do-it-upper I like the look of." He continued without drawing significant breath. "Production started in 1947 and..." Tracy began to regret asking the question, though Marty failed to see the slight raise of her eyebrow as he focused on the traffic and he continued his description all the way to their destination.

The job done they returned to the shop and a day that would produce no more clues to fuel Tracy's suspicions.

Chapter Five

It needs doing promptly

Back at the shop, Marty was again pleased at how Tracy was working, they had had quite a busy afternoon. Tracy was kept well occupied but continued to mull over her suspicions about what extracurricular activities Marty might get up to away from the shop as she worked. As she thought about all the signs it occurred to her that, given that she now knew something about the finances, the shop must be hard put to provide enough to keep Marty comfortable and pay her a decent wage; he had upped her pay after just three months when it was already apparent to him that she was "a natural" as he put it. Her feeling that he must be up to something increased further.

At the end of the afternoon Marty told Tracy that he would lock up and, after she had left, he spent a while sitting at his desk in the stockroom. Another little expedition was getting firmer in his mind. It had been differently conceived this time and was proving to have aspects to it that negated the term little.

George Godwin was a well-known figure in the criminal world. Marty was very much a loner, he never worked with others and did not associate with the criminal fraternity. However living as he did pretty close to the centre of London some signs of such a community were all around him so to speak and he did keep his ear to the ground. He had been in the Carpenter's Arms a pub the other side of the city in the East End of London. He was not a big drinker, here he had just wanted a quick one on the way back from a job, but he was a very good listener. It was while there that he heard the rumour. Godwin was going to retire, to move and take up permanent residence on the Algarve.

Marty reckoned that just prior to that there would be a variety of ill-gotten gains in his house there ready to be taken across the English Channel to his new home. He also reckoned that Godwin was not a man to tangle with, he was reputedly a nasty piece of work who did not tolerate anyone crossing him; there were even rumours that labelled him a killer. But the situation was tempting. The man certainly qualified as someone Marty would not lose sleep over robbing and he was known to live alone so a range of possible complications was ruled out by that. Given his quiet low-key in and out mode of operating it seemed a possibility. He would have to make sure, absolutely sure, that the man was out when he broke in. He certainly did not want a confrontation. He was confident of his usual care and that his intended visit would leave no trace.

He listed what he would need to do by way of research starting with a visit to the house, folded the scrap of paper into his wallet, locked up and made his way home; he had promised his wife a meal out that evening. He was feeling in a mellow mood and thought that he might treat her to Fredericks in Camden Passage just off Islington Green, an area well known for housing a variety of antique shops. It was not the cheapest eating place around, but a very good one in his opinion.

A few days later he was all set. He knew there were elements involved beyond his normal way of working, but he had it all organised and his confidence of success was high. He anticipated a clear run, but resolved as ever to retreat at the first sign of any trouble; not that he expected any.

"I might be a bit late tomorrow love," he said, over supper the night before he had scheduled to go to Godwin's house. Mary was surprised, she well knew about Marty's jaunts and had not expected another one so soon, she wondered if this time it was something different.

"What are you up to? It's a bit soon for another of your little expeditions isn't it?" Marty had never lied to his wife, he could have made something up, pretended that this was something else, but he was straight with her.

"Just a little extra. Be the last one for a while, I promise, but this one is time sensitive, it needs doing promptly or the opportunity will be gone. Enough said, okay?" Mary knew better than to press the point, instead she said:

"Whatever it is, I'm afraid I need the car tomorrow, I've promised to help Miriam moved into her new flat and I won't be back until quite late." Marty frowned and Mary went on.

"You told me the other day that your current old banger was up and running, so we'll both be fine."

Marty had indeed said that and the old Jowett – Mary had always called his precious classics "old bangers" – was running well, but he did not usually use one of his special cars on an expedition. Everything was fixed though and he did not want to delay. He reckoned it would be okay just once, it was not as if the journey was particularly lengthy. He was sure the old car would not let him down.

"Okay then love, it's no problem." If he had dwelt on it at all he might have thought that any change to his way of working could increase the risks he took, but the need to get the job done without delay before Godwin made his permanent move overseas was paramount. He still anticipated no problem and to begin with he was correct.

Chapter Six

Way outside his experience

It was close to two o'clock in the morning, George Godwin left his car parked on the drive just outside of his front door and retrieved his small suitcase from the boot. As he locked the car and walked up the steps to the door his movement triggered a light into action above it. He was tired after a long journey from Portugal, airports are nobody's favourite place, and he could not now wait until he was in his new permanent residence and the regular commuting between countries of recent times was done with. Right now he just wanted his bed. The next time he made the trip would see him move. Yet, weary though he was, when he opened his front door to find an intruder standing in his hall right in front of him, his response was well-nigh instant. He dropped his suitcase, which toppled away to his left and fell back down the steps, and his gun, retrieved from the glove box of his car and habitually in his pocket whenever he entered his house, was in his hand within a couple of seconds. His outrage at finding his home breached by an unknown stranger, who he presumed was stealing from him, was extreme. For a moment he fumed, struggling to speak, as the stranger stood unmoving with the shock evident in his startled expression. After a couple of seconds he found his voice.

"How dare you?" He spluttered, his voice rising to a shout. "What the hell are you doing here?" He believed he knew the answer to that of course and intended to do something about it. "Who are you? How did you get in here?" Everything he said was powerfully decorated with expletives.

Marty's mind was working overtime, though he found he was rooted to the spot and that the hall was now well lit as the outside light shone in through the open door. He had been sure Godwin was still in Portugal. He knew Godwin's reputation and, while he had known the nature of the chance he had taken, his checking had made him feel sure that he would not be interrupted. Godwin's trip had clearly come to an end early. Such a situation was way outside his experience; he might be a criminal but he had never been confrontational and this was the notorious George Godwin – so realistically Marty reckoned he was as good as dead. He wanted to protest, to shout out, to plead, but found his throat was clamped tight shut and little more than a croak emerged.

"Well, nothing to say?" Godwin's voice was now low and menacing as he took stock and decided what to do next. Doing so did not take long, he decided he did not really care who this man was, his breaking in had sealed his fate and he would soon be dead. Godwin did not linger for a single second on the morality of his decision nor did he worry about the disposal of a body; it was, after all, something he had done a number of times in the past. None had ever been discovered. However he did have one practical thought – he would avoid creating any mess in his hall; arrangements now made in Portugal meant he was about to get viewings of the house scheduled for prospective buyers and everything had to look smart for that. He had to move this intruder to... to the garage, he decided.

"Raise your hands and turn round," he instructed, his voice now slow, steady and spoken in a tone that brooked no argument.

Marty's heart was in his mouth; he was rightly terrified, and he struggled to get his breath. He might be crooked himself but he had never even touched a gun and this situation was way outside of even his wildest nightmares. He really had no idea what to do. For a split second he considered retaliating, but rejected that as suicidal and tried to think of an alternative to following Godwin's instructions. He gripped the torch in his hand so hard it hurt, he tried to think of any possible escape, but still nothing came to him and, as the seconds ticked away, Godwin spoke again.

"Move." It would be difficult to imagine any greater menace being encapsulated into a single word. In his panic Marty took a step forwards, and he did so just as Godwin did the same thing. The latter, now impatient as well as angry, intended to push the gun against his intruder's back and herd him through to the kitchen where a door connected straight on directly into the garage. Both men moved together at the exact same moment. Moving awkwardly Marty nearly lost his footing on the shiny tiles of the hall floor, he lurched forward a little as the two men collided, and as they did so the gun became sandwiched between them as their bodies pressed together with some force.

In that second the gun went off. The sound of the gunshot was muffled to a small extent by the two bodies pressing on it. Nevertheless the sound seemed deafening in the quiet hall and so close to him. As Marty felt his hearing deadened, he also felt the cold, hard outline of the gun against his chest and then the sensation of a warm liquid, which he realised could only be blood, soaking into his clothes and oozing down his front.

As his mind tried to take in that his last moment had come, George Godwin fell away from him and slumped to the floor. Marty took a step back and stared down at him finding that he was unable to move or quite believe that the blood he felt on his chest was apparently not his own. Godwin was quite still, he lay with one arm stretched out and with the gun remaining in a loose hold by his fingers. The silence after the gunshot was profound and a slight acrid smell created by the discharge lingered in the air. Marty stood dazed and unmoving for a couple of minutes as his hearing and breathing returned bit by bit to normal. A sudden loud click startled him, but it was only the over door light switching off. In the resulting gloom he shone his torch down, still somehow clutched in his hand, but there was still no sign of life from the crumpled body lying in front of him.

With the front door remaining half open still, Marty stepped to the threshold and peered out into the darkness, he found all was quiet; the shot had apparently gone unnoticed. He stepped out, triggering the light to illuminate again, and grabbed hold of Godwin's suitcase, he lifted it into the hall and pushed the door closed. He tried to force himself to think straight. After a couple of minutes the outside light, which he realised must have been controlled by a timer, switched itself off again. Marty swung his small torch around the room again settling the thin beam on the body. As far as he could judge Godwin appeared to be dead. Marty had never seen a dead body in his life and wondered how to check, he squatted down and felt one of Godwin's wrists for a pulse, then did the same to his neck, whilst not being quite sure exactly where to put his fingers. He also gave one of his shoulders a shove. There was no reaction and, as far as he could tell, no pulse. He shoved again; all the signs suggested that the man being dead was certain, it was perhaps unsurprising as a few moments before he had been shot in the chest at point blank range.

Marty stood up and took stock. He knew he had been careful during his clandestine visit, he had worn gloves and the kind of plastic bags that forensic teams wear over their shoes as he always did on a job, so he remained sure that there would be no sign of his presence in the house. He had picked a lock to get in, dealt with the alarm and closed the safe so there would be no sign of a physical break in. He could, he hoped, just slip away leaving no sign. Remembering the outside light, he changed his mind about exiting by the front door and went through the kitchen into a utility room that had a door out to the side of the house and which he judged would afford him a safer exit. Godwin was security conscious and the door had a good quality lock on it; it opened at a touch from inside and snapped back and locked as Marty, still being careful and quiet, closed it behind him. It would, he believed, give no clue to his use of it. It was dark outside and he had to feel his way round to the front of the house as his eyes got used to the lack of light, he came close to falling over a wheelbarrow but in a few more yards he was back on the road after exiting the property by a side gate. He looked both ways up and down the road, but no one was in sight and none of the nearby houses showed any lights. He pulled off his gloves and shoe covers and stuffed them in his pocket as he picked up his pace and walked back towards his car which, following his regular practice of keeping a distance from the scene of his crimes, was parked some hundreds of yards away and around two corners. He spotted the familiar humped shape of his old Jowett a few yards ahead of him just as a man on a bicycle pulled out from a driveway onto the road not far ahead of him. For a moment he stopped dead in his tracks, but the man turned away from Marty and did not look back as he cycled away. As he got out his car keys and opened the boot to put his bag in, a milk float, its electric drive almost inaudible until it was upon him, overtook.

"Morning mate, early start, eh?" For the driver to sound so cheerful at such an hour seemed absurd and his voice startled Marty who mumbled an acknowledgement at the departing vehicle as he worked the car key into the door lock and got into the driving seat. He had been facing the car so the dark patch of blood on his front could not have been seen, besides he was, as always, parked away from any streetlight.

The Jowett was running as if it had been manufactured yesterday, Marty's work on it had restored it well and, after all, the car had originally been built as a quality vehicle. He took several deep breaths and concentrated on the sound of the engine. He tried to focus on revelling in his good renovation work and the car's smooth running in an attempt to push what had just happened to the back of his mind, but it proved difficult, and his mind kept conjuring up an all too vivid vision of his narrow escape. He drove on and in less than an hour he had reached home, he put the car away in his lock up and just sat in the driving seat for a few minutes thinking of how easily things could have been different; he had come so very near to being killed. Again, he took a few deep breaths, left the lock up and walked the few hundreds of yards to his house. He no longer carried his bag, having paused to put that in his secret hiding place along the way; despite his normal confidence his careful nature meant he would never have the spoils of his expeditions at his house; besides Mary would never allow that.

He unlocked his front door and stood silent and unmoving in the hall for several minutes, still trying to calm himself down. It would be alright he told himself. He had left no sign of his presence in the house and there was nothing, nothing of any sort, to connect him with George Godwin who anyway was a man whose demise he reckoned many would not mourn. What he did have was a now sticky patch of blood on the overalls he always wore over his clothes for such work as he had been engaged in tonight.

He went into the kitchen, keeping quiet so as not to wake his wife, and stripped off most of his clothes. Some blood was also evident on his shirt and a little was visible at the top of his trousers. Doing the household's washing was not a usual job of his, but he did know where everything was, he put a detergent tab in the machine and sprayed the affected part of his clothes with a liberal amount of the stain removal that he knew Mary used for anything she referred to as stubborn; most often that applied to oily stains from his work on his cars. He selected a programme and wondered if the noise of the machine would wake his wife. He decided immediate washing was the priority and that the kitchen extension at the back of the house was sufficiently far from the bedroom to cause no problem. He pressed the on switch, retreated out of the kitchen and closed the door behind him. He was not even one hundred percent sure that he had left Godwin dead, though that was his belief, either way he hoped his subsequent actions would be the end of the matter as far as he was concerned. He crept up the stairs and slid into bed being careful to create no disturbance; his wife did not stir.

Back in Chigwell the body still lay unmoving in the hall a growing patch of blood now clear to see beside it; it was now a certainty that George Godwin would not be taking up his planned residence in Portugal.

Chapter Seven

Something that can throw some light

The morning of the day after what Marty regarded as his near death experience a solitary woman approached the back door of George Godwin's house. She let herself in with a key taken from her bag, took off her jacket, put on an apron imprinted with a bright coloured flower pattern and busied herself in the kitchen for a while assuming her boss was late getting up or had gone out early. She was in her fifties, Portuguese, and had been working at the house for a couple of years; she knew nothing of her boss's business, sometimes she found him there, sometimes not. They enjoyed what might be called a minimalist relationship; they talked very little, but Godwin had always been good to her and paid her a generous rate that he hoped meant that she was unlikely to leave and land him with the uncertain chore of finding a replacement. He had always appreciated her services and had been minded to try to pass her on to the houses' new owners when he sold up.

The kitchen was soon tidy, so she moved on following her regular routine, got together the kit she needed for the bathrooms in a square plastic bucket and headed off to make a start in the downstairs cloakroom. As she walked into the hall the presence of the body was obvious, lying as it was on an empty area of the hall floor, blood at once visible where it had spread across the tiles. She stopped dead in her tracks, gasped out loud, retreated several steps back until, finding herself against the stairs she sat down two steps up from the floor. She let go of the bucket and it toppled over spilling some of its contents out onto the floor. Faced with the sight of the householder lifeless on the floor her face had taken on an ashen hue and when she ran a hand through her hair, she misjudged what she was doing, dislodged a hairpin and let a loose lock escape.

After a few moments her shock turned to curiosity, she noticed the gun in his hand, and dwelt on the blood spoiling an area of floor that she polished with great care every week. She sat motionless for several more minutes without making a sound then got up, her movements slow and deliberate, and walked a little unsteadily into the living room. She had a thorough knowledge of the layout of the house and approached and opened the drinks cabinet and poured herself a generous portion of brandy into what she well knew was an expensive cut glass tumbler; she then downed it in one smooth gulp. Only then did she go to the landline phone in the kitchen, she dialled 999 and was promptly asked which service she required. Her English was not perfect, and her reply was concise.

"Whichever one right for someone shot dead." She said and directed the responders to the location of the event.

The police arrived within six minutes to find her sitting outside on the front steps, the front door open behind her and the body visible just over the threshold. An initial assessment was made by the two constables in the patrol car. They needed only a moment to decide that Godwin was indeed dead and that CID should be called for, and before long a detective inspector, a sergeant and, a little later, a pathologist arrived and began a serious examination. They knew the house and they knew its owner… and they liked him not one bit.

"Murder, do you think? He must have had plenty of rivals… and enemies too." The pathologist, a man shrouded in protective clothing and a facemask with only his eyes visible, unnaturally large behind strong metal framed glasses, was silent and Inspector Green continued: "so, murder, suicide, accident or what Peter?"

"Give me a moment, you well know this process always takes time and you know I have to be sure. There is no obvious sign of a struggle, but the autopsy will show more, some bruising perhaps."

"What about time of death?" The pathologist was crouched by the body, he stood up, pushed his glasses up his nose and gave Green a world-weary look.

"You know I can't be specific at this stage… but it looks like the early hours of the morning. More anon, okay?"

The inspector just grunted and turned to his sergeant.

"You've been round the house?"

"Yes, everything is clean and tidy and seems undisturbed, but it looks like Godwin's been away and the cleaner – she's the one that phoned it in - comes in once a week, she has a key to a back door. There's just two outside doors and I have checked both and been round all the windows, there's no sign anywhere of forced entry - maybe it was someone he knew… if someone else was here, that is."

"The suitcase?" The inspector had more questions.

"It's locked, but the label shows he had arrived off a flight. We can check that if necessary."

"Yes, do that. What about an alarm? Surely there is one?"

"There is, but it appears not to be switched on."

"That seems very unlikely, this is George Godwin we are talking about. Can you imagine him leaving his precious house unprotected? And I can't believe it was suicide. Is anything more improbable than that someone who's just put himself through all the privations of a long flight, stepping into his hall and standing and shooting himself within two steps of their own front door? It makes no sense to me, no sense at all. We must try to establish if someone else was here, it really does seem the most likely option. Let's go round the house again, complete the procedure to establish a proper crime scene, and then we can start the house to house."

They all regarded the necessity of house-to-house inquiries as a tedious business, in this case the likelihood of anyone being aware of anything happening in the early hours of the morning was unlikely in the extreme. And so it proved, that is until Sergeant James came across Elizabeth Gardener two doors down. Unlike many people, wary of time-consuming involvement or just plain unhelpful when faced with the police, she was disposed to be of assistance if she could.

"Now that you mention it I might have heard something. I was up in the night with my cat, Bella, she's not very well you know and needs medicine in the middle of the night. It's very inconvenient, it often takes me a while to get back to sleep again, but I had set the alarm so I know I was up at two and a little after that I did hear a sound from outside, short and sharp but not very loud, I'm afraid I paid it no great attention. Not much help I'm afraid, I didn't go to the window as it didn't seem to warrant investigation, so I can't say more. I'm sorry."

"That's quite alright Madam," Sergeant James was at his most polite, "good of you to spare us a moment, thank you." He turned from where they stood on her doorstep to walk back to the road.

"Perhaps you should ask Michael, he's always about at that time." She addressed his departing back and he moved to face her again.

"And who is this Michael?"

"He delivers the milk round here, bottled milk is making a comeback you know, it's very ecological." Now that might help. The sergeant asked her if she knew the company name and Elizabeth gave him her last bill, which was amongst a bunch of letters and papers on the hall table. He renewed his thanks and went back to the crime scene.

Hearing what he had discovered the inspector sent him off to find the milkman. Enquiries at the depot discovered the fact that he would by now have finished his rounds and be back home. An address was given, and the Sergeant then found him answering the door in his dressing gown and explaining that he was having a quick nap after his nightly rounds.

"How can I help?" He asked rubbing his eyes and looking less than enthusiastic at having his sleep disturbed by the police.

"We are investigating an incident that occurred in the small hours last night." He gave Michael an address and asked: "Were you anywhere near there at, say, well between one and three o'clock?"

"Yes, I guess so, it's on my round."

"Well, did you see anyone, anyone at all? It's a quiet neighbourhood so anyone moving about would surely have stood out."

"I don't think so, no, there's usually not a soul about; the kind of people who live in an area like that tend to keep regular hours. I usually see more cats than people, and foxes too, for that matter, but let me think." The Sergeant let him take his time and after a moment's thought he continued.

"I saw a few cars, but only in the distance, other bits of my round are in busier areas, but, hang on, one thing I remember now, I spoke to someone, just to say a good morning you know, I passed right by him as he was getting into his car at the kerb. I think I made him jump. The electric milk float is virtually silent, see. I didn't notice his face, he had his back to me, but I remember because of the car. It was old, unusual, a Jowett I think's the name. Rather before my time, I would need to see a picture to be sure."

"Did you get a registration number?" That was most unlikely at night but the Sergeant asked anyway.

"No, it was parked with cars in front and behind it and I doubt the number was visible at all or that I would have noted it."

"Can we sit down for a moment? If I look the car up on Google you can check a picture to be sure."

Michael nodded and led the way to the kitchen and they sat down, the Sergeant got his phone out and began a search. Within a minute or so he showed Michael a picture. A Jowett it was confirmed to be, a car with a distinctive shape and a long sloping back, a Jowett Javelin.

At the end of the day Inspector Green and his Sergeant were back in the inspector's office at the police station comparing notes."

"I still think suicide is most unlikely, none of the circumstances seem to point to it; doesn't seem like him either. Someone else has to have been there. What have you got Mark?

Please tell me you've found something that can throw some light."

"Well, we seem to have what might be confirmation of the time of death, the cat lady heard what could have been the shot and she's sure that was just after two in the morning. Otherwise there is only one other bit of information that might help." He opened his notebook as he spoke. "That milkman, Michael something or other, he only saw one person out and about in that area of his round at the right sort of time, he didn't see his face, but he was getting into a car parked at the kerb and the car was, I discover, most unusual; something of a classic. It was a Jowett Javelin, not a make I've come across, but it was quite a prestige model back in the nineteen fifties and sixties it seems. I reckon you have to be quite an enthusiast to own a car like that. I've checked it out and what's more there are very few examples of it left that are registered and running. If we start with the London registered ones we may be talking about a very small number."

"Okay, it's getting late, get on to that first thing tomorrow would you, it might turn out to be someone who saw something. We should have the pathologist's report then too." As he spoke there was a knock at his half open office door and the pathologist's head appeared around it. He had shed his protective clothing and was dressed in casual wear, in jeans and a neat V-necked pullover.

"Can I come in?" he asked.

"You can if you have any useful news for me."

"Not yet, you know it's still too soon, but... ah, I see, you were being sarcastic. Nevertheless there is one thing I've found, and I reckon this should narrow the search to a considerable extent." He held a small plastic evidence bag up in the air and gave it a waggle.

Chapter Eight

It seems a fair assumption

Marty was up at his usual time the following morning, he was first to go downstairs and he emptied the washer/dryer of his clothes and was relieved to see no trace remained of the blood. He had thrown away his gloves and shoe coverings on the way home and was content that he had done all that was necessary to cover his tracks. He was still shaken though, he well knew that he could so easily have been killed and, from what he knew of George Godwin, if that had happened his body would just have vanished without a trace forever. It was a sobering thought, he knew that the job had rather different to his usual way of working and he would, he reckoned, have to think with some care about the nature of his future expeditions. He realised that all through his previous career, whilst he had always been careful, he had also been lucky. He never wanted to be in that sort of situation again; he might be a criminal, but he was a mild mannered man and found exposure to a higher level of criminal activity had been a real shock to his system. It was a moment that would linger in his memory for a very long time.

He composed himself as Mary came into the kitchen and gave her a cheery good morning.

"Hello love, everything alright?" She replied as she put on some toast for them.

"Yes, thanks, no problem," he said adding, "I wasn't very late so I thought I would crack on into the shop as usual this morning." A small lie designed to reassure, and he hoped she really had been asleep when he had got into bed. She did not question what he had said.

"Tracy opens up if she's there first these days doesn't she? By the way, have you got things organised for her anniversary? You need to look after that girl; she's proved a real gem over the last year."

Marty acknowledged the comment with a brief word. He might not discuss the details of his extra curricula expeditions with Mary, they had always been agreed on that, but they had always conferred about the shop and she well knew and approved of what he planned. They chattered on normally enough over breakfast though Marty could not get the previous evening's experience out of his mind, he gripped his mug tight and was conscious that his heart was still racing faster than usual. Then Mary asked about the car.

"How did your old banger go?" He was relieved to be able to focus on something different.

"Actually, very well. I've done a good job on her I reckon, it may be time to sell that one on and look out for a new project. I should make fair a profit too - and it's *not* an old banger, certainly not now, it's a Jowett." They grinned at each other as the old banger reference was something of a running joke between them.

Breakfast finished Marty set off to work, he was a few minutes late and Tracy had already opened up when he arrived, and she was busy cutting a key for an early morning customer. They exchanged greetings over the buzz of the key cutting machine and Marty went to his desk, still mulling over the events of the previous night. He went over it all minute by minute, trying to be logical, and could not see any likelihood of his presence in the house being detected, he reckoned he had been his usual careful self. But he could not help worry, a death surely meant the certainty of an investigation and... he tried to put it out of his mind and thought instead about the forthcoming anniversary of Tracy's employment. He had plans for that and he read over again the note he had written to her setting out a revised working arrangement for the future, a note intended to confirm the key details of a chat he planned to have with her on the day. Content that it did the job he intended he put the envelope back in his desk drawer to await its being handed over on the due date.

After a busy but routine morning Marty went to get a sandwich for lunch and picked up the midday edition of the *Evening Standard*. He sat in the café for a while and as he turned a few pages of the paper he found a story about Godwin pretty much as he expected: *East End Villain found dead in Chigwell*. The story was short, there was a bit of background about George Godwin, much about him was rumour and speculation, but he had form, had been in prison and he was described as being *a thoroughly nasty piece of work*; he had not been, the paper said, *someone to get on the wrong side of.* Certain past crimes he was suspected of carrying out were mentioned during which the perpetrator had not been shy of resorting to violence. About his death little was said: *found lying dead in his lavish home in Chigwell... recently returned from Portugal... a shooting... suspicious circumstances.* The piece ended with the bland and traditional phrase: *police say inquiries are ongoing.* Inquiries Marty found himself hoping against hope that would not involve himself, and would peter out in short order as, Marty thought, the police would be happy to see the back of George Godwin. Not that they would ever say so in public. However Marty reckoned that now Godwin was dead filing the matter away was perhaps their closest option to convicting him and throwing away the proverbial key. Surely that was what they would do. Marty put the newspaper aside and resolved to put it all behind him.

At the end of the afternoon Marty congratulated himself on having immersed himself in the day and not let dwelling on the affair with Godwin that had almost cost him his life distract him. Little did he know that there were those not far away who planned for it to cost him his freedom.

On the fringes of London Detective Inspector Green took stock with his team.

"So, we are no clearer as to how Godwin was shot but, after some checking, the evidence we now have shows without doubt that there was someone else there and that there is a clear candidate for that someone: one Marty Holmes. We don't know why he was there, he has no form, that's been checked, but given his work as a locksmith it seems a fair assumption that he was there to steal, I imagine he would have had little problem getting in. Perhaps he was disturbed and shot Godwin to escape. First thing tomorrow we go ask him."

Chapter Nine

Clearly something serious

At nine o'clock on the dot Tracy opened up the shop. Now she had worked there for nearly a year Marty totally trusted her and was starting to hand over more and more; he was not always as prompt at the start of the day as he once had been. Tracy was. She had learnt a great deal from Marty, and had long resolved to fit in with his way of working as much as possible; and he did regard punctuality as a virtue. The shop needed to be open as stated on the door. When she thought about it she realised that she was a different person these days to the disgruntled girl packing cardboard in a supermarket best part of twelve months ago. She turned the door sign to "Open" and went straight through into the stockroom and clicked the kettle on, as it began to make bubbling sounds, she heard the shop bell ring and the sound of what she assumed was the first customer of the day stepping inside.

She headed out to take up a position behind the counter and was faced with two men, both wore grey suits and the taller of the two held out a small booklet, snapping it shut and removing it again so fast that she could not see it properly.

"Police." The man spoke in a clipped and firm tone. "Is Mr Holmes here?"

"No, not yet."

"When do you expect him?" It was all very formal, and it was also, she found, somehow a little intimidating.

"Wait a minute who exactly are you? What do you want? And how do I know you are police?" The tall man again replied.

"I'm Detective Inspector Green and this is Sergeant James." He again held out his warrant card. Tracy was wondering what to make of their presence and wondering too what Marty had been up to; after all, to the best of her knowledge you don't get an inspector and a sergeant on your doorstep merely for an overdue parking ticket. Maybe her suspicions about her boss's activities could be right. She found herself playing for time.

"I've never seen one of those before, you could have bought it in the market for all I know."

"I think you know very well it's real, come on now tell me your name."

"It's Tracy, Tracy Hines."

"And you work here, yes?"

"Yes, I do. Have done for nearly a year now. I'm doing a sort of apprenticeship. Do you want me to prove it, I could cut a key for you if you like." The Inspector's face hardened into a glare that expressed no amusement and he glanced at his sergeant before continuing.

"That won't be necessary, but a bit more cooperation will be. Tell me, does your boss own an old car, a Jowett Javelin?" Tracy relaxed a little, maybe this was only something routine about the car, she had resolved to say as little as possible, but the car ownership was doubtless easy to check so she saw no harm in confirming it.

"He does yes, it's his hobby, he does up old cars, classics he calls them. Why?" At that moment she saw Marty outside on the pavement, the shop bell rang as he opened the door and the policemen turned towards the sound. They went through the police and warrant card bit again and it seemed to Tracy that Marty looked pretty rattled. He acknowledged that he was Marty Holmes, but otherwise remained silent, though, had she known, he was already fearing the worst.

"Tracy here tells me you own an old car, a Jowett Javelin, is that right?" Marty had no idea where this was going but, having finished his renovations and taxed the car to allow it to be legal to drive on the road, like Tracy he knew that this could be checked in moments.

"Yes, I do. I renovate old cars, it's a hobby. The Jowett is the latest. What's this all about?"

Tracy interrupted, "I asked that. They wouldn't tell me."

The Inspector gave her a stern look. "Cooperation remember," he said and turned back to Marty as she decided no purpose was served by her joining in, though, finding her instinctive reaction was to be protective of Marty, she gave the inspector what she hoped was her best defiant glare.

"And were you driving that car in the early hours of yesterday?" In an age of widespread surveillance and with traffic cameras lining so many streets in profusion Marty had no difficulty deciding that it would be imprudent to lie about that, though his mind was working overtime. It seemed certain that this related to George Godwin and the reason he had driven the Jowett out to Chigwell. He wondered what to say, finding as he paused, the Inspector pushing the point.

"Well, were you?" Marty thought fast and found he had an answer.

"Sorry. Yes, I was. I've just pretty much finished my renovation and wanted to give the car a test run at a time when I wouldn't get embroiled in traffic. That's not a crime and I'm pretty sure I didn't break the speed limit." The inspector gave him a long stare; he somehow had the air of a cat about to spring on a lame mouse.

"Perhaps not, but it's what you got up to when you parked up in Chigwell that I'm interested in. I think you better come with us. We need a word and that needs to be done down at the station." Marty looked grey, he rested his hand on the counter as if for support. However he decided not to resist, it was clear that these two would not take no for an answer and he still thought he had left no evidence behind at Godwin's house to incriminate him. Instead, he drew himself up to his full height and turned to Tracy.

"Looks like you will have to manage the shop for a while, Tracy, look after things for me… and ring Mary and tell her what goes on will you?" Tracy couldn't think of anything to say, this seemed to be anything but a routine matter, but she nodded at him to show she would do just that.

"Where is the car kept?" The inspector asked Marty and was told about the lock up round the corner. After that the sergeant put a hand on Marty's arm and guided him towards the door, they turned right, disappeared from Tracy's view and walked together through the market, the packed street being a traffic free road Marty presumed any waiting police car was parked somewhere beyond the end of the market road.

The shop seemed very quiet after the three men had left and Tracy stood for several minutes almost unbelieving of what had just happened. It seemed clear that something serious was going on, and certain that Marty was in some sort of trouble, and again she wondered if her suspicions about him were well founded. After a moment she snapped into action, she reversed the shop sign to "Closed", locked up and headed out to Marty's home to speak to Mary. She reckoned this news was something that needed more than a text or a phone call. As Tracy hastened out of the market to speak to Marty's wife, the police arrived at Marty's lockup.

"Open up." The Inspector's request was abrupt and Marty unlocked and swung open the door. The car was parked next to the shop van, its back to the open door all just as normal. The sergeant checked the registration number against something written in his notebook and exchanged glances with the inspector.

"That looks like it," he said, and addressing Marty added: "Right you, we need to get you to the police station for a serious talk."

"What's this about? I've said it's my car and told you what I was doing."

"There's more to it than that, we'll talk more when we get there." The inspector allowed him to lock the doors then ushered him out from the cul-de-sac and towards the police car parked a little way down the road, which they had got into at the end of the market and used to drive the short distance to the lock up. Marty said nothing but his fears increased and were compounded by wondering what Mary's reaction would be when Tracy spoke to her. He was very conscious that the Godwin expedition had been a little different from the norm. He was soon sitting in the back of the car as the sergeant drove, the journey to the police station seemed to be taking them towards the North East and away from Islington. It was not what Marty expected.

"Where exactly are you taking me?" He asked.

"Loughton," came the monosyllabic reply, to which Marty protested that that was miles away.

"It's our base. If you don't want to make a journey, you should stick to committing crimes on your own patch." Marty began to protest that he didn't know what they meant, but he saw it was useless and relapsed into silence. No one spoke during the rest of the journey. Marty did not try to get them to explain further and the police offered nothing more by way of explanation. Marty sat in the back of the car, a picture of misery, as he envisaged his whole life about to unravel. They seemed to know more than about the car, but what? They must know something that led them to believe he had been up to something and that could only involve the death of George Godwin. Yet he had been so sure he had left no trace at the man's house. He found his hand was shaking and clasped both hands together tight as the London streets moved past the window.

"What are you doing here at this hour?" Mary was surprised to see Tracy visiting the house during shop hours, especially as the shop had not been open long. Tracy had hurried to the house, knocked on the door and asked if she could come in. Mary held the door wide and Tracy walked past her and headed for the kitchen, the traditional terraced house had a large kitchen extension at the rear. Mary followed her in.

"Now what's all this about? Is Marty alright?" She had by now assumed a worried expression, having decided Tracy's unexpected visit could only mean there was some sort of problem.

"Yes. No. Or rather, he's fine but I'm afraid the police came to the shop this morning before he arrived. He walked in on them and there's clearly some sort of problem; they were asking questions about the car – you know the old Jowett he's been working on – it appeared to be linked to the car being seen in Chigwell late at night. Marty said that he took it for a test run late to avoid being snarled up in traffic. Seems reasonable; I know he was pleased to have the car at the up and running stage. But the police would say nothing more, they seemed pleased that he admitted to the car business and took him in for questioning. He said to tell you and I thought that ought to be done face to face. That's all I know."

Mary sat very still for a few moments then got up and clicked the kettle on. She knew enough to connect his driving the Jowett late at night with his recent little expedition. It was a situation she had feared at the back of her mind for many years, but of course she knew no details of what Marty had been up to and had no way of judging the seriousness of the situation. She gave nothing away to Tracy as she asked:

"Do you want a cuppa, dear? I guess we will just have to wait and see. I wonder what the silly old bugger has been up to."

"Yes, okay, a quick one though, I mustn't leave the shop closed and unmanned for too long." Mary made tea and placed the two mugs on the worktop of the breakfast bar, Tracy thanked her.

"I am sure it's nothing serious, he'll probably be on the phone soon saying it was all a big mistake." Tracy rather doubted that even as she said it, but felt she had to say something that sounded reassuring. Mary took a slow sip of her tea, thinking that it almost certainly was about something serious, and worrying about just how serious Marty's role in this particular something might be.

"Well, as I said, we'll just have to wait and see. Will you be alright at the shop?" She knew full well that Tracy was more than competent to cope and her face betrayed the fact that her question was a deliberate attempt to change the subject. If Tracy went back to the shop she would not be facing any more questions for the moment. Tracy assured her that she would be fine, she finished her tea in a couple of gulps, they assured each other that they would make contact if there was any more news and Tracy walked back to the shop and reopened it for business.

She heard no more during the morning from either Marty or from his wife. But in the middle of the day Sergeant James reappeared unannounced at the shop. He turned the door sign to "Closed" as he came in and snapped the lock.

"I need you to answer a few more questions," he said. She at once tried to find out more about what was happening.

"What's all this about, surely I've a right to know?" That the sergeant disagreed was clear: he would only say they were engaged in what he referred to as "routine enquiries", a phrase he clearly knew told her nothing. He pressed on with his questions.

He asked about her role in the shop and Tracy, who saw no harm in talking about that sort of thing, repeated that she was an apprentice, she played down her role somewhat, saying nothing about the more complex jobs, safes and the like, that the business entailed, and countered all the sergeant's questions about Marty with the minimum amount of information she felt would be acceptable to him.

"I have been to his house a few times and I know his wife Mary, but I've no idea what he does away from the shop, and before you ask I don't work here at two in the morning. As far as I know he spends most of his free time at his garage, old cars are his absolute passion. Nothing wrong with that surely. What's all this about anyway?" She tried again to find out more, but again to no avail; it was clear that the police were not prepared to give anything away, something that somehow made her fear the worst. Sergeant James had formed the view that Tracy was just an assistant serving at the shop counter and concluded that he should not regard her as a useful source of information.

"Can't say more, not while inquiries are under way. I suggest you keep your head down and mind the shop, I don't reckon you are going to see that boss of yours for a while, maybe for a long while." The sergeant adopted an ominous tone for this last observation.

His departure was as abrupt as his arrival and, after his last remark, Tracy found herself at once fearing the worst, that Marty was some sort of crook and that it was that which had caught up with him. She found she preferred the word rogue to crook. As Mary had said they would just have to wait and see. She turned the door sign back to "Open" and got back to work.

Chapter Ten

Good news or bad

It was turning out to be a busy day. Maybe once a month Tracy took turns with her mother to cook a proper lunch at home and have a real break. An occasional longer break was something Marty had encouraged saying that sometimes a change was due to their usual fare of snacks and sandwiches in the middle of the day. She realised that today was such a day, and today it was her mother's turn to cook. Their stormy relationship of recent years had almost all evaporated following Tracy getting what her mother described as a "proper job", a description that most often linked to the phrase "at long last". Even so Tracy still had hopes of getting her own home, a difficult thing in a location so centrally located in London.

She always picked up the evening paper for her mother on her way home, she took little notice of it as a rule but today she got the lunchtime edition of the *Evening Standard* on her way to the flat. The meal, she was told, was going to be a little while as her mother had been later getting in from her work than she planned. So she thumbed at random through the paper as cooking was being finished.

A few pages in the heading of one story jumped out at her: *East End Villain found dead in Chigwell*. Chigwell: it could not be a coincidence, the place had come up in the police questioning and it seemed to be where Marty's car had been spotted the other night. Given that, she found her suspicions were hardening, Tracy would not have been that surprised to notice a burglary linked with Marty's situation, but a killing was something she certainly did not expect. That seemed really bad, though from all she knew of Marty from almost a year of working closely with him there was no way she could imagine him as a killer. It was all a great puzzle, and she had no option but to follow Mary's suggestion and wait and see.

There was a photograph of George Godwin alongside the story, the poor quality of its image increased the impression given that this was not a man with whom to mess. Was there a link there, she wondered, and if so just what had Marty been up to that night?

"Okay, the food's on the table, get your head out of that paper." She responded to her mother's summons but said nothing to her about her fears as they chatted over their meal. She would hear something soon enough, the market was a breeding ground for rumours, but what those rumours would be in this case was another matter. After their meal Tracy's phone buzzed as it received a text from Mary, its message was brief: *No news yet.* She replied equally briefly reiterating that they should keep in touch.

Lunch over Tracy was again back in sole charge of the shop. She had done that plenty of times before, of course, but the reason this time made it seem odd and she continued to worry about Marty. She wrote Mary a text asking to be kept updated, then deleted it thinking that she was overdoing the checking, she was sure Mary would say when there was any news. Then she got an emergency work call soon after she had returned from lunch: someone wanted to get access to a safe following someone's death. Assuming it might be something she could do unaided, a trip out seemed to be on the cards.

"Do you know what kind of safe it is?" She asked, trying to find out if she could cope with it or if it was a job that must wait for Marty's return; she knew that in such circumstances many potential customers might go elsewhere if they did not get a quick response.

"I've no idea, sorry." Not a very illuminating or helpful reply. She asked if the safe had any sort of label on it but the man was not in the late safe owner's house and so that drew a blank too. She warned them that in that case it might take two trips if they wanted it opened in a way that left it undamaged and able to be used again. Discovering that that was not regarded as a problem she gave them a rough estimate of cost and arranged to meet the caller at the house in half an hour's time. The address was not far away. She gathered the tools she would need and set off to get the van in time to make the rendezvous. She used the second key to the lockup that hung on a hook close to Marty's desk.

By some miracle she found and parked on an empty meter, she located the house nearby and rang the doorbell. She had no real idea if she could do the job, but she really wanted to get it done if possible and be able to tell Marty she had done so. The door was answered by a woman.

"Good afternoon, Holmes & Son. I'm not the son, I'm Tracy. I arranged to visit on the phone."

"Do come in." The woman, a middle aged one with a distracted air, ushered her in. "Thanks for coming. It was my husband who phoned, it's his late mother's house, he's not here, but he reckoned you might need some identification and so on, I guess you can't go round breaking into any old safe someone points you at, can you?" Tracy acknowledged the fact that she could not and scanned a number a documents she was shown, including a death certificate for a Moira Jones. She was pretty sure everything was as stated.

"So, where's this safe then?" She asked and was taken upstairs to what appeared to be the main bedroom, where it was apparent that a clear up was under way as the bed was littered with piles of clothes; it looked like some lucky charity shop was about to have a field day. Built in cupboards lined one wall, a couple of doors stood open and a safe was visible at floor level, bolted she assumed to the floorboards from its inside.

"How long will this take do you think?" Tracy glanced at the safe and gave her what she hoped was a reasonable estimate.

"Okay, do you mind if I leave you to it for a little while? I need to pop out, just up the road and back, okay?" Tracy agreed, despite feeling that it was rather odd for her to be left alone in the house. Nevertheless she prepared to check it out and heard the front door close as she did so. Looking at the safe again, she found that it was indeed nothing special and she was pleased to discover that she knew it was a job she could do. She got out her tools and set to work.

Well within the time she had indicated she had the safe open. She had drilled through the door and the lock, a straightforward combination one, was destroyed. The safe could not be used again but they had the quick access they wanted, one less thing to worry about in what must be the mammoth job of clearing and sorting a whole house following someone's death. She looked out of the window which faced the road, but there was no sign of her client returning, so she sat down on the mattress of the stripped bed.

Inevitably in such a pause she thought of Marty and wondered what was happening. She had heard no more since Mary's last brief text. She checked her phone but there were no more messages. Had he been up to something that had drawn the attention of the police and did it link to the death in Chigwell reported in the evening paper? As she wondered about it she looked at the safe, the door now standing ajar. She wondered what was in it. There was no sign yet of the woman returning, maybe she could look inside. She got up, knelt down and swung the door wide open. The contents of the safe appeared to consist for the most part of documents, though there was also what appeared to be a jewellery box. As she pondered this she heard the front door open and a voice called up the stairs.

"How's it going up there?"

"Just done," she replied, "do you want to have a look?" Footsteps on the stairs answered her question and the woman appeared on the landing and came into the bedroom.

"There you are then, the door's open and you can get at things now. I'm afraid the safe won't be useable again, but I did tell you on the phone that would be the case."

"Sure, yes, that's fine, there's just so much to do and that's one little job out the way, thank you. Can I settle up? Did my husband agree a charge?" Tracy confirmed the amount, which more than covered her time as the work had proved to be straightforward.

"I'll make you out a receipt," she said reaching into her bag for the book and a few minutes later she exchanged it for a cash payment and went back to the van; she had timed it well, the parking meter had less than ten minutes left on it. She was pleased the job had been no problem, and pleased too that she would be able to tell Marty about doing it on her own – and she hoped that would be something she could do soon. As she drove back to base she thought about the nature of her work: alone in that house, a safe full of who knew what, it was without doubt a job that sometimes came with temptations. The woman, and she suspected her husband too, appeared to have no idea what was inside the safe. Goodness knows what she could have made off with. What a thought.

She housed the van away back in the lock up and arrived back at the shop just in time to squeeze in cutting a key before closing time. Then, as she reversed the door sign to "Closed", her phone pinged: she had a text. Assuming that it was from Mary or Marty that could mean good news or bad she thought as she pulled her phone out of her bag to check.

Chapter Eleven

We know you were there

Once at the police station, Marty found himself left sitting alone in a featureless interview room for what seemed like an age. There was little to take in: two chairs set either side of an old and scratched table with a recording device on it where it abutted the wall and not a lot more; the walls were bare and in need of a coat of paint and an elaborately constructed spider's web decorated one corner of the ceiling. The window was set too high to see out of from a sitting position and was far too small to create an exit route, the whole room could have done with a comfort rethink. Described in one word 'bleak' would probably suit it best. Alone with his thoughts Marty tried to think about how to play things. He had after all been out on a job and they had clearly identified the car, so there was no point in denying that he had driven to Chigwell. However he was still confident of his precautions in the house and felt that there was little chance he had left any clues to his presence inside, but even so he was worried. This was, after all, a wholly new experience for him.

He had survived many years of having stealing as a side line, it was less that he had chosen the activity, more that it had chosen him: it was like a family tradition he had been bound to take on, first working with his father and later continuing on his own. And he had proved good at it, but he was finding that he was not anything like as good at this sort of thing. He noticed his hands were shaking a little and pulled them off the table into his lap, clasped them together and told himself he had been left alone in a room doubtless intended to be drab and to put him on edge and make him feel vulnerable. He reckoned he could only try to brazen it out; he took a couple of deep breaths and found it did not help to calm him. Not. One. Bit.

After what seemed an age the door opened and the same team that had brought him to the station came in, sat down at the table, and gave him meaningful looks. In the moment's silence that followed Marty tried to take the initiative.

"Is one of you going to tell me what this is all about?" He said, trying to keep his voice steady, he considered asking why he had been brought all the way to Loughton instead of to his local police station, but decided it was pointless, that was no doubt how the system worked. The inspector ignored him as he set up the recorder and announced who was present in the room.

"I would rather you told us, Mr Holmes," said the inspector at last. "Let's start with why you were in Chigwell the night before last shall we?" His tone seemed to stress the difficulty of the situation and Marty glanced at the red light on the recorder, a sign he took to remind him to be careful about what he said, though this question he felt he could answer in a way that sounded convincing.

"I told you: I renovate old cars, classic cars that is, it's a hobby, something I've done for many years. The latest one, the Jowett Javelin you've seen, was ready to go on the road – it's recently taxed and insured – and I took it for a run late to avoid getting snarled up in traffic." As he repeated his story he still reckoned it sounded like a reasonable and convincing explanation. He considered asking how they knew about the car, but decided that would not help. He just again added a question: "What's this all about?" The inspector ignored his question and continued with his own.

"Do you know a George Godwin?" This brought Marty up short, though after all he had already presumed it was Godwin's death that had prompted this. His first response was truthful.

"If you mean the George Godwin who is known as something of a villain, then no, I don't know him. I am only vaguely aware of his name from the newspapers."

"Strange thing is he was shot and killed in his home on the very night that you drove to Chigwell; in fact, you parked pretty much round the corner from his place."

"You can't think I had anything to do with a shooting? That's just not…" Marty's instant denial was interrupted as the inspector spoke again.

"No, we don't think you were there, we reckon we know you were. In fact we are absolutely sure of it." Marty's heart raced, the situation was getting worse and worse.

"That's ridiculous. I don't know the guy, and I have never touched a gun in my life… and why on earth would I want to kill him? He sounds like someone most people would give a very wide berth to." Marty still felt he was making sense, though he found himself getting more rattled by the moment. At this point the inspector suggested they break for a while.

"It will give you time to think." He said, promising to organise some refreshments as it was approaching lunchtime. Marty found that being left alone was almost as unnerving as the questioning and that both the sandwich and the coffee he was brought were disgusting. He did not know that during the break Sergeant James had been back to Islington to have a few further words with Tracy. After what seemed an age the two policemen returned as did the questioning. Sergeant James revived the recorder and the glowing red light reappeared.

"So… you *were* there, and Godwin is dead, what was it, a falling out amongst thieves perhaps?" The inspector had spoken the statuary interview starting details into the recorder again and continued to pursue his previous line.

"I was in Chigwell, yes, I've told you that, but I certainly didn't kill this Godwin man, I didn't. I had no reason to, I …" Marty's voice faltered and as he realised, he had not denied breaking in or being a thief the inspector interrupted him again.

"Let's be very clear shall we. We know you were there. You describe your old car as a classic, right?"

"Yes." Marty's response was a reflex. "It's a great car, they were all the rage in the fifties and sixties, it..." Again his voice failed as the two policemen looked at each other and exchanged a smile.

"Okay, you don't need to try to convert us to becoming classic car enthusiasts, I agree it's a classic. Never mind the fifties and sixties, do you know how many of those cars are still around and registered today?" he gave Marty no time to think, never mind answer. "Very few. And the number of them registered to addresses in the London area is vanishingly small."

"So?"

"So, I must say that it's beyond coincidence that such a car is parked near a break in and shooting and is owned by, guess who... a locksmith." It was getting worse, Marty remained silent, and the inspector went on to make matters worse still.

"Not only are we sure you were in Chigwell, we are sure you were in the house. Not that you left a trail of broken locks or anything, you are clearly skilled at your trade or whatever you call it. Show him the evidence Sergeant." Sergeant James reached into his pocket and produced the small clear plastic evidence bag that the pathologist had given to them the previous evening.

"Do you know what this is?" he asked, his voice harsh and confident. Marty squinted but could make out nothing in what appeared to be an empty bag. He shook his head, his mind in a whirl as he tried to imagine what might be coming next.

"As you know George Godwin was shot dead. His body was found in the hall of his house, lying on a nice clean polished marble floor, in fact his body was found by the woman who regularly cleans it." Marty could see he was stringing this out; and that he was enjoying so doing.

"Do you know what was alongside the body?" Marty didn't know and he didn't say anything. The inspector let the silence hang in the air for a long moment.

"No, you probably don't know. But you made a mistake. It appears you struggled with him and…" It was Marty's turn to interrupt"

"No, I didn't, I…" But he was not allowed to get any further, the inspector had the bit between his teeth now and was intent on finishing.

"It was a scuff mark on the marble, a smudge from the black rubber sole of a shoe, and one that contained some specs of dust, not just any old dust. It's metallic dust of the sort that comes from cutting keys. I reckon you should sweep your shop floor a bit more often if you are going to go out killing people." He paused and gave a contented look, his delight with the thought that they had cracked a high-profile case so very quickly clear to see.

"I very much think we have got our killer, eh Sergeant? Anything to say now Mr Holmes?" Marty was stunned, he thought back, the plastic shoe coverings he had worn must have split when he collided with Godwin. They were convinced that he had killed the man; they believed it was all wrapped up. He found himself at a complete loss. His head was spinning, and he found that his mouth had gone dry, something he put down to the long difficult day.

"I, I… can I have some water?"

He had started to reply but felt sick and instead played for time. The inspector said nothing, then nodded to his colleague who got up and left the room. Neither Marty nor the inspector said anything for the two or three minutes that then elapsed before the sergeant returned with a glass of water. Marty took a sip. His head was spinning. The only thing he could think of was that he was at a pivotal point in such an interview. He had to get help, in fact he now thought that maybe he should have insisted on that much earlier.

"You've got this all wrong. I think I want a solicitor. Can I phone my wife and arrange that I…" He didn't finish the sentence, rather his voice faltered a little and, in what seemed like slow motion, he slid off the chair onto the floor where he lay motionless.

Chapter Twelve

Sorry, it's an emergency

Exchanging a brief glance at each other, in no time both policemen moved onto their hands and knees alongside the prone figure of Marty. He was not unconscious; indeed he was struggling to get up as they came level with him.

"What's happening...? I feel I'm..." Marty's voice was a little slurred and as he turned towards him the inspector noticed that the left side of his face seemed a little twisted.

"Bloody hell, it looks like he's had a stroke." The inspector at once reached for his mobile phone and summoned an ambulance, he well knew that if it was a stroke then an urgent response was essential. He knew too that there was not much a layman could do, only artificial respiration if necessary, but Marty seemed in no need of that, his breathing if anything was heavier than normal. Green was as sure as he could be that the man was a crook and in all likelihood a killer too, but for now his medical needs superseded everything else and he did not want anyone dying in the station on his watch with all the complications that he well knew would be sure to follow from such an incident. He hastened to reassure Marty as he and his colleague helped him get up from the floor and back sitting on the chair. Marty lowered his head to rest on his arms on the table.

"Help is on the way, now you stay still." Not much reassurance but it was all the inspector could come up with. He shouted for help, more people came into the room and he got one of the team to go to the front door ready to guide the ambulance crew directly through as soon as they arrived.

In an organisation such as a police station many emergency actions are usually well-rehearsed and systematic regimes, and such was the case here. Marty found himself largely unaware of the detail, but he was lucky an ambulance arrived in just a few minutes, the crew, a man and a woman, checked him over and verified that he seemed to have suffered a stroke; they administered an injection before taking him to the ambulance.

"Tell my wife, tell Mary..." Marty's plea, was clear enough, although his voice remained a little slurred, and what he said was heard by both the ambulance crew and the police.

"What do we do?" Sergeant James asked his superior, knowing full well that in most circumstances sick prisoners were not as a routine allowed visitors in hospital. It was something of a harsh rule and often caused problems as anguished relatives tried to rebel against it.

"I guess we tell her. After all the man's not under arrest, we were still at the stage of his agreeing voluntarily to be questioned, you better go and see her, we can do without any complications, that girl in the shop may well know where you can find her. She may well work and the shop address is all we know right now, the car is registered to that address too. And get a constable to go with the ambulance, I don't want that man left alone."

As the sergeant hastened away the inspector cursed under his breath. It was clear to him that they had been only an inch or two away from solving a murder, and doing so in record time too, something that was sure to be regarded as a good result; now this. He cursed again out loud and muttered under his breath "Just a few more questions." But for the moment more questions would have to wait.

Soon Marty was put inside the ambulance and was on way to the nearest suitable hospital. He was aware of the siren, which helped the vehicle push through the traffic, even in this hectic age such sirens were heeded by most drivers and they made good progress, although the journey seemed to him to take a long time. He was aware too of someone bustling around him and, as his head lolled a little, a woman's voice spoke close to his ear: "Stay awake, stay awake."

Marty began to take in what was happening to him better once he was in hospital. First he was whisked along a network of corridors on a trolley, a journey that include going up in a lift. Doctors and nurses then fussed over him and the doctor who appeared to be in charge told him he was in Whipps Cross Hospital and that he appeared to have had a stroke.

"Lie still and relax. We'll need to do some tests to help us assess your condition. Try not to worry. Be back in a moment." Marty looked around him, he was in a side room rather than a ward with a police constable sat in the corner and a nurse was stood at the end of his bed filling some detail in on a clipboard of what he presumed were his notes.

"Nurse?" Marty beckoned her towards him, she slipped the file into a receptacle at the foot of the bed and came alongside him.

"Don't worry Mr Holmes, you're in good hands, we'll take care of you. Is there anyone I can call for you?" Marty's voice was a little stronger now.

"Yes. Please. My wife." He struggled to get the number out but the nurse was able to make a note and headed out of the room. Constable Short, who at six foot two was always known as Lofty, was not sure what to do, he didn't know if the circumstances permitted visitors. He felt he should check and went out into the corridor to make a call. He was not the happiest of constables, having been reprimanded twice in the last month for being too heavy handed, and now he had been landed with hospital guard duty, something every police officer always regarded as a real chore and boring to boot. Through to the station he was told Holmes's wife had been informed and with something of the circumstances explained he steeled himself for a tedious day, he couldn't help thinking that the man in the bed was not going anywhere in his condition; it seemed clear that a guard was unnecessary. He would have nothing to do but brood about his own problems. When the doctor and nurse returned to check on Marty the doctor brusquely ushered the constable out of the room.

"Put that chair outside the door please, Nurse. I want this man to try to relax."

Constable Short found himself banished, the doctor's tone had not seemed one he could resist. Such duty was tedious at the best of times, now he could not dredge even a little interest from what went on as he could not hear what was being said. He pulled out his phone and within minutes had allowed himself to log into a gambling site. It was the last thing he should be doing, he knew that, he was in very considerable debt already. He resolved to limit himself to ten minutes.

Checks finished the doctor again promised Marty more information to come. As she left the room the nurse, whose badge identified her as Beth smiled at him.

"I'm sure Mary's on her way", she said and smiled at him again. She had been told by the constable that the police were in touch with his wife but made what she hoped was an appropriate and comforting remark and one she believed to be true.

When Sergeant James arrived at Holmes & Son again, he was not greeted with any pleasure. Tracy glared at him.

"You again, what do you want this time? Where's Marty, what's happening, or can't you say anything but 'routine enquiries'?" Tracy let her anger, uncertainty and worry sound in her voice. And she got an answer albeit it was not one she wanted.

"Calm down, I need to speak to his wife, it seems he's had a stroke and is in Whipp's Cross Hospital, do you know where I can find her?" Tracy blanched.

"Is he okay?"

"I have no idea how serious it is, just tell me where I can find his wife." Tracy glanced at her watch, thought for a minute and concluded that she knew where Mary would be.

"Well you won't find her at home, she'll be working. I'll take you – she's helps out on a stall at the other end of the market. Come on." Tracy grabbed her bag, came round the counter, changed the shop sign to "Closed" and followed the sergeant out into the still bustling market. She locked the door, waving away an intending customer who was almost on the doorstep.

"Sorry, it's an emergency,"

She rushed through the market ahead of the policeman ignoring the greetings and calls of the many curious stallholders she now knew after a year of working with Marty. Mary helped on her friend Jill's stall, which sold pet foods. Tracy called out as they approached.

"Mary, Mary!" Mary looked up and replied.

"What are you up to, who's minding the shop?" Then she saw the policeman; even out of uniform it was well-nigh impossible that any member of the police could walk through such a market and not be recognised. "What does *he* want?" she added with a snarl. Tracy glared at the sergeant and took the lead.

"Mary, I'm so sorry, you need to come at once. They think Marty has had some sort of stroke, he's in Whipps Cross Hospital." Jill, her colleague on the stall, had heard what was said, she caught the apron Mary took off and threw to her and waved her on.

"Go! Go! I'll manage closing up."

Mary told Tracy to come too, her voice brooking no argument, and they followed the policeman to his car. He clicked his key fob to unlock the doors, then opened and held open the back one for them.

"For God's sake man, just get in and bloody drive will you. If I'm too late to see him I tell you now you better watch out for me." Once under way she calmed a little and asked what he knew about his condition, which of course was less than nothing.

"What's he doing out at Whipps Cross? I thought you took him to the police station down the road." The sergeant explained that he was involved in a CID inquiry and that Marty had therefore been taken to the police station in Loughton that was their base. Tracy noted Mary's controlled fury, this was not an irrational rant – it was clear that there was a formidable woman side to Mary's character that Tracy had not seen in their previous occasional informal and social contacts. Mary did not pursue the question of Marty's condition, but kept up a regular series of comment about their progress.

"Put the damn siren on, for God's sake, if he dies while I'm in traffic you're going to wish you'd never been born" was the least of it. Mary clutched Tracy's hand in a grip tight enough to turn the flesh white as the blues and twos sped them through the London traffic and they made good progress.

On arrival at the hospital, they got directions without hassle, it seemed Mary was expected, and they were hastened to the lift by a porter and then on towards the ward alongside which Marty was being taken care of under the watchful eye of Constable Short. The sergeant, having pointed them in the right direction, did not accompany them further. Marty had been relieved to hear Mary was on her way and had been struggling to work out what to tell her. He had no more medical knowledge that the next man, but he did know that once you have had one stroke the chances of having more increased and that a second one could sometimes come in quick succession. It was a sobering thought, one made worse by the fact that it seemed that the police believed that he had killed Godwin, imagining some sort of falling out amongst thieves as it were. He reckoned that Inspector Green had been on the verge of charging him with murder when he had been taken ill. If he didn't make it he could not have Mary thinking forever more that he had killed someone, he would have to tell her what happened. He just prayed the policeman who was again sitting in the corner of the room, and whose instructions were to keep an eye on him, would allow them some privacy.

A few minutes later the door opened, and Mary came into the room with Tracy at her heels. For a second they both took in the unfamiliar surroundings, then Mary stooped over him and kissed him on the forehead.

"You silly old bugger," she said "you've given us all a right scare, how are you? What have the doctors said?" Her words tumbled over each other in her haste and in her relief at seeing him alive and sitting propped up in bed.

"I'm feeling a bit better now, love." He paused and whispered and she bent to hear. "I must tell you something, but..." he indicated the policeman sitting bored and uncomfortable in the corner. Mary turned from the bed and walked towards the uniformed man. Even in the confined space of the small room strode would be a better description.

"Right you, out. Out, out, out! Give the man some privacy for goodness sake." She stood over him.

"I have to remain with him, I'm told there are still questions to be asked by my colleagues in CID."

"I'll have some questions for your colleagues in CID if you don't clear off. Is he under arrest?" The question was greeted by a sheepish look.

"No, not as such."

"No, I didn't think as much. So go, go now or…"

The man was already rising to his feet as Tracy had her 'Mary's a formidable woman underneath' theory confirmed. Constable Short did not want the hassle. He reckoned she was right, no arrest - no supervision. He went and took up his station outside in the corridor musing on the fact that he had no great love for CID, it was not his case and that he just hated hospital guard duty. In any case he had other, more pressing, things to worry about. Mary sat down next to the bed and Tracy got hold of the chair that had been vacated by PC Short and pulled it into a position a little behind her in the narrow room.

"Right love, what needs saying?" They both gasped out loud as Marty said:

"They're trying to pin a murder on me."

Chapter Thirteen

Just in case

"What? What do you mean a murder?" Mary looked horrified, but her look soon softened as she added: "That's nonsense right? You couldn't hurt a fly, love, I know that." Marty was aware of Tracy in the background, but he couldn't cope with processing what that meant, he just wanted his wife to know he had not killed anyone.

"You know that, but they think otherwise. I have to tell you what happened, I might not get another chance if I don't get out of here."

"Don't be daft, the doctors say he expects you to be fine." Mary had been given a brief report by one of the nurses as they had been directed to the room.

"We'll see, I do feel a bit better, but anyway you know I was on a little expedition don't you love?" Mary just nodded as Tracy took the expression to give the definite impression that such things were plural and that they were not secret from his wife; her suspicions seemed to be correct. She remained silent and listened.

"Well, I'm usually so careful, so very careful, you know that too." Again, Mary nodded and put her hand on his arm to reassure him in what looked like a long-practiced gesture.

"This time it was different: I knew it was a bit more risky than normal, the house belonged to George Godwin, you know, now in the news, I expect. I had heard he was moving abroad and reckoned he'd have stuff stashed away ready to take with him. He's a right villain, not someone I'd worry about hurting, now he's dead and just fodder for the newspapers. But it might have been me got killed. It bloody nearly was."

"What do you mean, love? What happened?" Mary again had a look of concern on her face.

"He walked in on me, didn't he, straight from the airport and back from Portugal he was. I was at the front door just about to go out when it opened up and in he came. Face to face in an instant we were. The whole thing only took a moment, he had a gun out in seconds and threatened me with it, he meant to do it too, kill me I mean, I know he did. He was more than capable of murder, in fact I don't think he gave it a single moment's thought. Anyway, he told me to turn round, I admit I was terrified, I thought my last moment had come. Not thinking straight, in my panic I took a step *forward* just as he did the same. We collided, the gun was squashed between us and… it went off. That was it, next moment he was lying dead on the floor. One panicky step saved my life. I didn't hang about, I scarpered out of there pretty damn quick I can tell you."

"Thank God it wasn't you got shot," said Mary, "but that wasn't even self-defence, it was an accident."

"I know love, but I reckon they are so delighted to have found out I was there that they just want to pin it on me. A murder all wrapped up in a few days is just what will do careers some good, you know. And no one else was there."

"We'll get legal help, it will be alright, you'll see. How do they know you were there?" Mary asked and Marty told her the details about the car and the metallic dust in the scuff mark and told her that, given that, his presence in the house had been impossible to deny.

Mary had been concentrating on Marty, hanging on every word, and worrying too given his stroke and the tale he told. Now as she paused and took stock she realised that Tracy had heard everything too. She twisted in her chair to speak to her.

"You'll say nothing about this to anyone young Tracy, right?" Tracy had no difficulty framing a reply nor in refusing to believe that Marty had killed someone.

"You can be sure of that Mary. Marty you've been really good to me, I reckoned you changed my life, besides I believe you and those policemen are right bullies. Not a single word, I promise." Mary nodded and seemed satisfied, she reckoned they had got to know Tracy pretty well over almost a year and she believed she meant what she said.

"There's something else..." Marty looked past Mary to Tracy as he spoke, and she knew what he meant.

"Let me give you a moment. I'll see if I can find us some tea." Tracy slipped out of the room to hunt some down ignoring the constable sitting outside in the corridor who appeared lost in some game on his mobile phone as she passed him.

"Okay what else is worrying you? And anyway you mustn't worry, what happened can't possibly be made out to be murder, you'll see. Once you are up and about again we can..." Marty interrupted his wife.

"That's just it love, you may be right, I hope so, but a single stroke always increases the chances of another, it may not be as easy as we hope. So, will you do something for me?" Mary replied that of course she would do anything and used the word anything with great emphasis. Marty continued to explain his fears.

"It's about the shop, Tracy will keep that going just fine, I'm sure, but I have to be realistic, just in case I don't get out of here or need to recuperate for a while, I want her to see what we planned, you know, will you tell her? You don't have to explain, just tell her that there's an envelope addressed to her in my desk in the stockroom. Everything's all set out. Okay?" Mary agreed to direct Tracy to the note, which in any case had been due to be given to her in just a few days' time.

As they chatted on Tracy returned with tea for them all, but then a few minutes later the doctor entered the room.

"I think maybe that's enough excitement for him for the moment Mrs Holmes, we should let Marty rest, will you come and see him again tomorrow?" Mary said she would, and she and Tracy got up to leave. Mary gave him another kiss, Tracy gave a little wave and assured him she would be fine coping with the shop and he should not worry about that. Mary paused at the door and looked back.

"Bye love, see you tomorrow. Let's see what a new day brings, eh."

Chapter Fourteen

This isn't over

Hospitals tend to get things on the move early and on the morning following Marty's admission to hospital Inspector Green was there soon after eight a.m. knowing that Marty Holmes should be able to speak to him uninterrupted at that time if that was allowed. He arrived in an unmarked car driven by his sergeant Mark James. He waited in the car while the sergeant got a ticket to park having decided that the last thing he wanted was to get clamped. Ticket in place on the dashboard they went inside, bypassed the main hospital reception and went straight up to the ward. These days most ward entrances have security locks on them and their knocking was answered by a nurse. She wouldn't let them in and allowed a conversation only through a narrow crack as she held the door open an inch.

"Police. We need to speak with Mr Holmes, he's here in a side room."

"It's not visiting hours and I'm afraid I have no idea whether Mr Holmes is fit to see you. I must ask the doctor. Please wait a moment." This was voiced with just a hint of resentment, it seemed like a well-rehearsed response to unexpected visitors and there seemed no way round it. Warrant cards and the mention of a murder enquiry which the inspector had added in at the first hint of resistance made not a jot of difference. She shut the door and disappeared walking back through the ward. After a few minutes, which Inspector Green spent pacing the corridor, his frustration clear to see, a doctor appeared from the ward and asked what they wanted.

"We need to speak to Mr Holmes, Doctor, it is important, I wouldn't ask otherwise." His attempt at politeness was, if it was in fact intended, a failure. The doctor, who had been interrupted on his morning ward rounds, expressed the view that this would not be a good idea.

"Mr Holmes is still unwell; he did have a stroke yesterday you know." The inspector now pressed the case to the point of rudeness.

"I'd hate to see you hindering a murder enquiry Doctor, surely just a few minutes would be alright?" The doctor agreed, his manner indicating he did so very reluctantly just to end the conversation; he specified a time limit of ten minutes. As he led them to the side room, he called to one of the nurses.

"I want these two out in ten minutes, please Nurse, and not a moment more, you hear?" She nodded, came forward and held the door open for them.

"These two gentlemen want a word Marty. The doctor's said no more than ten minutes, okay?" It seemed she meant the question rhetorically as she didn't wait for a reply and was gone in a moment. Marty was sitting up in bed, he had been awake since about six o'clock and was ready for a snooze.

"What do you two want? I can do without you harassing me." The inspector said nothing as he settled himself in the only chair, his sergeant left to stand, the constable who he had favoured with the briefest of nods as he passed, was sitting just outside the door. The door had been left open ajar, allowing the constable to hear what was being said and, given that he had been told little or nothing about the case, he hoped it might add some interest to his solitary and boring vigil.

"Well, Marty, may I call you Marty?" Inspector Green continued without waiting for an answer. "What I really want is to arrest you for the murder of George Godwin. Not that anyone will miss him, he was a nasty piece of work and no mistake. The world is doubtless better off without him. But I suppose arrest may have to wait until you are back on your feet again, nevertheless I would hate you to think we've forgotten about you." Marty tried to ignore him though he realised that he was not about to go away, at least not until he had had his permitted ten minutes.

"We know you were there, the evidence of that is conclusive: first that funny old car of yours and then the metallic key grinding dust. Why don't you admit it?" Marty felt he had to say something and hastened to state his case, the urge to deny an accusation of murder proving to be irresistible.

"Alright, I was there, I had broken in. I reckoned he was a nasty piece of work and deserved it. I thought he was in Portugal. I would never have been there if I thought there was even the slightest chance of his being at home. Did you know he was moving overseas?" The inspector nodded and Marty went on to explain what had happened, stressing that he was the victim and that both the collision with Godwin and the gun going off had been an accident. He used Mary's phrase: "It wasn't even self-defence, it was an accident. I was lucky not to be shot, that's for sure what he intended. But for one step made in panic I would be the one left dead." That said he had a sudden thought: "I was in the house only two or three minutes, I didn't even have time to find a safe never mind open it." He was not going to admit to theft. In fact he had been so shaken up as he fled that he did not yet know anything much about what he had got away with; the spoils were stashed out of sight in his secret hiding place.

Now Marty had given an explanation the inspector's reaction was clear on his face: it was not what he wanted to hear and moreover it was something he looked unprepared to believe. He glared at Marty as he saw his case becoming a little less certain.

"More likely this was a falling out amongst thieves and you murdered the man." Marty decided he couldn't cope with any more of this and got angry.

"No, no. You wait till I get legal representation, I'm not even sure what this interrogation is, you're not recording anything, it's turning into a vendetta. I'm saying no more." He stretched out his arm to reach along the edge of the bed and his hand found the red call button. He gave it a long press and soon a nurse, who he saw was Beth, the nurse who had helped him when he had first been admitted, was at the door.

"Get rid of these people, I can't cope with it. Please." The nurse knew the situation and chased them out with a firm few words.

"It's obvious Mr Holmes is not up to this, you must leave at once. Now please." Feeling it inappropriate to argue and very much annoyed by the course of the last few minutes the inspector signalled to his colleague that they should leave and went out of the door, making the briefest of comments: "This isn't over" and then, seeming to be unaware of the cliché, adding: "I'll be back." Before leaving he spoke as well to the constable, just two brief words: "Watch him."

Beth gave Marty a big smile. "Alright now?"

"Yes, thank you, and thank you for your help last night, I reckon I was in a poor old state. And by the way, if you've heard I'm a murderer - it's *not true*, I would never hurt a soul."

"I'm sure you're right, try to rest now, tests results are due back this morning and the doctor will see you again once the results are in. Who knows? We may have you out of here very soon." Medical staff are all trained not to get involved in this sort of thing, a patient is just a patient, but if asked she would have said she believed Marty was telling the truth. She smiled again and Marty found he rather hoped she was on his side.

Chapter Fifteen

This is difficult

Soon after Marty had his encounter with the police in the hospital, Tracy arrived at Holmes & Son to open up for the new day. Doing so took a while longer than usual. As she walked through the market she was accosted by many of the stallholders asking questions and wanting to know "what goes on with Marty?" The market was a close community, most people working there knew each other, many were friends, most lived around the immediate area and it was an environment in which news, and rumour, travelled very fast. Furthermore a good many of the people there reckoned to be able to spot a policeman at a hundred paces, uniform or not, and a few of them had no reason at all to be keen on them. Tracy accepted that all the enquiries were well meant; Marty had worked in the market all his life and he was a popular figure. She did not want to be unhelpful, yet felt she should not say too much. After acknowledging and brushing off many questions she paused close to the shop and spoke to Bernie, who ran the fruit and veg stall situated right outside it. She settled on confirming that Marty had been taken ill while being questioned by the police, but pleaded ignorance about the details and promised to pass on more news when anything was known.

"I'm just waiting, Bernie," she finished. "Most people recover from strokes, don't they, I guess we'll know more soon enough." Bernie grinned at her and Tracy suspected that she detected a touch of admiration in his voice as he no doubt wondered just what Marty had been up to.

"Sly old dog, that Marty. Who'd have thought, eh, and they say it might be murder." Tracy resisted pitching in with a denial and just said "We'll probably know more soon enough, I just hope he's okay." As she opened the shop door she knew that her acknowledgement of there being a problem would be round the market in short order. Nearby in the market another stallholder, James Boon, had heard this exchange. He did not know Marty, but he had seen a possible opportunity.

Yesterday's events had left Tracy with a great deal to think about. Her vague suspicions about Marty and his extra curriculum activities had at first been an almost humorous private aside to her work, though she did rather like the idea of his being a rogue of some sort. Her wonderings were now proved to be all too true. She did not know the full background, but it seemed clear from what Marty had said that he had broken into this George Godwin's house out at Chigwell and that while in the house Godwin had been shot. The report of his death seemed factual enough, the newspaper would have checked and not got that wrong and she'd heard Marty's explanation for it. She made a mental note to pick up the lunchtime edition of the *Evening Standard* to see if any further details of the incident had been reported.

Although she had had her suspicions, she was still somewhat surprised by the revelation. Marty had been very good to her, he was a mild mannered man and she had never gleaned the slightest hint from his character that allowed her to believe he was a murderer. A bit of a rogue maybe, but she was convinced no more than that. The shop bell rang and she greeted a customer and began another routine key cutting job. As she worked on it her phone pinged to announce the receipt of a text. Once she had done with the key, and collected the customer's payment, she opened up the message:

Marty wants you to see what he planned for your anniversary. Envelope in desk drawer. After you've read it meet in cafe 12.30.

It was from Mary.

She went into the stock room and found an A5 envelope in the drawer with her name in bold capital letters on the front. She returned to her stool, so that she was ready if anyone came in and opened it up. Inside was a garish coloured card with the word "Congratulations" on the front. Inside Marty had written:

A whole year at Holmes & Son. Well done you! You have proved to be a real asset and I hope there will be more to come (years that is). See note. Cheers.

His name was a huge sprawl below the message. He had, she realised, been keeping it for the exact day which would be the coming Monday. She held the card for a moment and reflected: she had worked for a year in a job she had found she liked more than she had ever dared to hope, she had learnt a great deal and was doing a greater and greater range of work on her own. It suited her, and she liked Marty, they worked well together, she was certain he was no more than a bit of a rogue and she had no intention of that stopping their association.

The shop bell rang, the unexpected sound interrupting her thoughts. Once the customer, a man intent on purchasing a padlock for his shed, had gone, she turned to the note folded inside the card. This was typed. He began with thanks: he was pleased he had chosen her… she had done well… she was a natural with locks… such a great help. He wanted, he wrote, to encourage her to stay in the business. No problem she thought, she wanted to stay, besides what else was she going to do – go back to a life of cardboard boxes? And Marty made specific proposals, writing:

I intend to make the shop operate as a partnership. We can change the name to Holmes & Hines, repainting will spruce up the shop front too, something that's long overdue. I suggest you continue to get a guaranteed wage, but we'll share the profits in future to give you more. There's details to work out, Mary will help with that. Hope you like the idea...

The huge swoop of the word 'Marty' was scrawled underneath. As the import of the brief message sank in, she made a mental note to show him how to spell check a document: (guaranteed was typed as garrantede). Then she stood up, her slow rising morphing into an exuberant punch of the air as she let out a loud whoop. Even through the closed shop door a woman at the fruit and veg stall just outside in the market heard and gave her a smile and a wave. Tracy was delighted, thinking that a 'proper' job, had just got even more proper if there was such a thing. She had said nothing to her mother about the business with the police, though she was bound to hear about it from talk in the market so she would have to tell her something in due course, though not the details about which she had sworn to keep secret. However, her job news she wanted to share at once and she sent her a quick text:

Promotion at work. All good. Talk later.

She just wished this development was happening with Marty busy in the shop with her rather than lying in a hospital bed; she hoped very much he would be alright.

Right on time Tracy walked into the café – she well knew that the words 'The café' in Mary's text meant the greasy spoon they used for almost all their breaks – to find Mary already sitting alone at a table in the corner by the window.

"I got you a sandwich, cheese and tomato, I hope that's alright." Said Mary as Joe, the white aproned mountain of a man who ran the place, plonked a mug of tea in front of Tracy with a cheery "Hi there, love." This being his traditional greeting to all his regulars male or female. He wiped moisture off his hands, swiping them down the front of his apron as he retraced his steps to the counter. Tracy voiced her thanks to his departing back and turned at once to address the important matter of Marty.

"How's Marty doing, have you heard any more from the hospital?"

"I phoned and spoke to a nurse first thing, she reported that he is getting a bit stronger, but they also insisted on reminding me that another stroke is a possibility. If there is another then it most likely comes soon after the first. I googled it too, so I'm not relaxing yet. Meantime we have this police business to worry about. You heard all that yesterday, right?" Tracy's voice was measured and slow, due for the most part to uncertainty about what she should say about something she was sure Mary regarded as a private matter.

"Well... yes, yes, I did."

"This is difficult, and it's something you might never have known about at all, but I have to be straight with you Tracy, truth be told my Marty is a bit of a tealeaf. I've always known about it, even before we were married. He's damn good at it too, we've been married best part of thirty five years and he has never been caught, never even been suspected. Mind you he doesn't do it that much, just the occasional little expedition – that's what we've always called it – and he has a strict code. He only ever steals from people he feels are wronguns, he's very strict about that, this is – I know it sounds odd – but it's like a family tradition, he followed in his father's footsteps you know. Anyway that George Godwin is... was, rather... that's for sure, a very nasty piece of work by all accounts. Quite a few people will be well glad he's gone. But there's no way my Marty's a murderer. It's just not possible." She had been speaking in a low voice, glancing around now and then to make sure no one was listening, but people around them were all lost in their own affairs and the general chatter and noise in the café made sure nothing was audible to others. But her voice rose on the last sentence and on the word 'murderer' and she paused for a moment." Tracy echoed her low tone.

"I agree. Nothing, absolutely nothing I know about him suggests otherwise. No way. He's a good man, I assume you know what's in that note he wrote to me, right. How good is that then?" At this point they were interrupted by someone entering the café and enquiring after Marty. Mary replied briefly and continued her conversation with Tracy.

"Yes, yes, I do know, of course I do, and you deserve it. I'll help work out the details. Marty and I have always talked about the business but not, well, not the other business, see. I never asked anything about what happens on his late nights out. I always knew when he was off on one of his little expeditions, but never any details of what it involved on the night as it were. Afterwards we never said more than 'all go well?' and 'yes, dear' – not ever. Best that way he always said." She paused again and looked out of the window, where the ever-busy market was going about its business.

Resuming in her previous tone Mary continued.

"But… this is difficult too. About his note to you that is. He's not getting any younger and he wanted to make this change – you know, to involve you more – before he began to slow up a little, take more time out. Now… well it occurs to me, given what's happened, what's going on, you may want nothing to do with us anymore." Tracy did not need to take time to think for long about that, speaking again after pausing just long enough for Mary to wonder what was going to be her response.

"No way, I've said I'm convinced he's not a murderer, his explanation made sense to me yesterday and it stills rings true with me now. I believe him. I'm more than happy to look after the shop while he's... well, away. Once he's fit again and the police thing is out the way we can talk about any new arrangement."

"Now he's in this mess, I suppose I always realised that something might go wrong one day, but I never thought... anyway that's another matter, right now I'm more worried about his health. I'll visit him later and see how he is – I wish he was nearer home, having to trek all the way to Whipps Cross wondering how he is, I don't like. What a mess. I must find out what we can do too, you know with legal help and all that."

"Yes, okay. Thanks, keep me posted. I better get back to the shop, if I neglect that you will want to fire me not promote me! And if there is anything I can do you say, anything at all, right?" Mary just nodded and waved Tracy away. She stood and walked back to the shop, fending off more questions as she went. She thought she had seen a tear in Mary's eye and her slow pace reflected the fact that she had much to think about. She opened up the shop, displaying the 'Open' sign, and almost at once got a call out, when she returned from that, standing at the door to the shop, someone was waiting for her.

Meanwhile as Marty lay in bed at the hospital he had thought up new worries.

Chapter sixteen

Something for you

Marty was still not feeling at his best, he was well enough to be bored and not well enough to want to do anything much but lie in his hospital bed. Although he was still in a side room he could hear the bustle of activity around about in what the noise indicated was a busy ward. The conversation he had been forced to have with the police earlier in the day had unsettled him. Worse than their not appearing to believe him, they appeared not to *want* to believe him. As he lay brooding about it he reckoned that Inspector Green just wanted George Godwin's death to have been a murder and for him and his team to have made a significant and quick arrest; for his own reasons therefore he did not appear to be prepared to regard anything else as a serious explanation. He seemed to have marked Marty down as crook, and thus someone who deserved everything he got. As he mulled all this over, ever conscious of the police presence just outside his room, the doctor arrived again.

Dr Amir appeared to be professional and kind, he wore a white coat, had a stethoscope around his neck and looked like he had not slept for a week. But like so many staff in U.K. hospitals he had to cope with a heavy workload and this was added to on a regular basis by a mix of emergencies and various staff absences, which meant that the ward always seemed to be overworked and under staffed. Marty had undergone a variety of tests, something of which he had only a vague awareness of in the fug he had been in when he had first been admitted. Now it seemed the doctor felt he could make a proper statement about Marty's condition.

"You're a lucky man, Mr Holmes," he began, "You had quite a bad stroke, but it seems to have left you with no serious aftereffects. Knocks you for six though that sort of thing and I expect you are still feeling weak." Marty acknowledged that he was.

"That should pass quite quickly all being well but, and I know I have said this before, but there is always an ongoing likelihood of further strokes and you need to be careful. It says here that you are a non-smoker, is that right?" Marty found he remembered answering that question and other similar ones about his lifestyle at some earlier stage, but his recollection was somewhat vague.

"Yes, never have been a smoker."

"That's good, I'll get the dietician to talk to you about things – it all helps you know. All being well we'll have you out of here before too long." He paused, glancing at the open door. "I see your... err, watcher is still here."

"Yes, he is, it's all a big mistake though and the buggers just won't listen, I only..." The doctor interrupted.

"Sorry, I'm afraid I mustn't get involved, my concern is solely for your health. I'm sure it will all sort itself out though. Try not to worry." He at once saw the look his last comment produced on Marty's face and added: "I know that probably isn't easy in your current situation but getting in a state is not going to help you one tiny bit, okay? Is your wife coming to see you again later on?" This last question drew a thin smile from Marty, and he answered with one word: "Yes."

After the doctor had moved on in his rounds Marty dozed a little, but hospitals are noisy places and, with his worries disturbing him too, his somnolent state did not last for long. Soon his mind was working overtime... the problems about his health and his situation combined to get him thinking about what seemed to be the very real possibility that, despite what the doctor had said, he might well not be going to get home anytime soon. If he did not have another stroke then it seemed certain that he would be arrested. He felt that neither was an attractive prospect, and each had one similar implication.

He mulled all this over for a while and then found and rang his call button. The nurse, the one whose label told him she was called Beth and on whose list he seemed to be, appeared at his door within moments. Having no great experience of hospitals he marvelled at those working in them. Beth seemed to him to be not much older than Tracy, yet she had massive responsibility and if he did take a turn for the worse he had no doubt that she would know exactly what to do and do it well.

"Are you okay? What is it?" She asked, a look of concern crossing her face.

"I feel much the same, thanks, sorry to bother you, but I need to write someone a note, I wonder if you can find me a pen and some paper… and an envelope too if that's possible."

"I don't see why not, I'm sure I can find you something in one of the offices. Give me a few minutes, eh." Marty thanked her and spent the next few minutes thinking about what he wanted to say.

Almost as soon as she had left the side-room the nurse got caught up in more medical matters – readying someone for an urgent trip to the operating theatre - and it was a while before she returned with what he wanted. She placed a pen, paper and a couple of envelopes on his tray table.

"Sorry that took so long, it's frantic out there today, well the fact is it's frantic every day. Here you go: there's plenty of paper there, I raided the tray in the nearest photocopier." Marty thanked her and she hurried off again no doubt to attend to more medical matters. Before he could get organised to write anything Mary arrived, she scowled at the constable sitting outside the door, brushed past him, shut the door behind her with a bang, gave Marty a kiss and sat down.

"Well, how have they been treating you, love?"

"Not so bad, except those wretched police were here again this morning. Eight o'clock, no less. They are intent on pinning something on me, I reckon, and then a few minutes ago the doctor told me not to get het up or I may have another stroke. Fat chance. Otherwise... no problems. You? And what about Tracy and the shop?" Mary had spoken to the nurse, Beth, on her way to Marty's room, and she too had suggested keeping him calm. Easier said than done in the circumstances, she thought, but she did have some good news to impart.

"Well, I do have something for you, Marty, a couple of bits of good news. First off you mustn't worry about young Tracy. I had a good chat with her. She is entirely on your side, says there is no way you could be a murderer and that she will say nothing out of place that might suggest otherwise to the police. She says you're a 'good man' and she's delighted with your plans for the way the shop is to be reorganised. We can work out the details on that between us all when you are out of here. Sound good?"

"Yes, yes it does. She's a good one that, I was right to take a chance and hire her. What else?

"Okay, I've been doing some checking. You know old 'Bodger' Bullen on the market?" Marty raised an eyebrow"

"Yes, a bit. He sells tools and stuff, I've sometimes bought things I need for the motors from him, but he's much more of a law breaker than I will ever be, got something of a record too, hasn't he? I keep a bit of a distance."

"He is also the one person I know who has had someone represent him in his dealings with the law. He gave me a number and I have spoken to a Howard Martin, sounded posh – and smart. If you need it you have a legal advisor all lined up ready and waiting."

"Well done you. Sadly I expect I'll need it. Did he say anything useful?" Mary continued her tale.

"He said it was complicated. No great surprise there. There were no witnesses to what happened, after all, so apart from your say so how that Godwin fellow met his end might be regarded as murder, manslaughter, self-defence or just an accident. He said Godwin's reputation should very much support your story though and he says any real plan for your defence must wait until we know what line the police will take. And… he also said you're not to worry, and, yes, I know that's not easy. Come on, let's leave all this for the moment, eh, tell me how you're feeling."

"Alright I suppose, I just can't stop thinking about it all. I was bloody lucky not to be killed but it's all landed me in a right old mess. I didn't touch the gun and I know it was Godwin's but I bet there's no way of proving it was his. It's all a right muddle." Mary tried to her best to calm him and they talked of other things for a while until visiting time was at an end.

As Mary left, she noticed that the constable who had been sitting outside the room had gone, replaced by a female officer who looked as disgruntled by hospital guard duty as her predecessor. She looked away as Mary passed.

Constable Short had spoken very few words to his replacement as he handed over, his mind remained on more personal matters as he hurried back to the police station and changed out of his uniform. He checked to see when his next shift started, he needed a little time and he had to think. He rejected the idea of going to the station canteen, the last thing he wanted was to get involved in small talk with any of his colleagues. He walked out of the station and continued along the road outside with no clear intention as to his direction. He passed shops without seeing them as but a blur and he didn't spot the man following him at a careful distance, but after some distance he did spot a café, a Starbucks, and decided to pause there as he decided what to do. It was mid-afternoon and the place was not too busy, he was able to go straight to the counter and order a coffee. After the obligatory lengthy dialogue about the precise size and description of coffee he wanted they asked his name and pointed him towards the collection point.

He stepped aside and stood deep in thought, so much so that they called out his name three times before he heard and took notice. Having collected his drink he found an empty table and sat down. He had only been there a moment when a man sat down opposite him and put a tall glass of coffee down in front of himself. Short glanced round the room.

"There's plenty of space in here, do you have to sit there?" Short spoke with a clear indication of irritation in his voice. Then he took stock: even sitting down as they were Short could tell that the man was an inch or two taller than him; that made him a giant of a man and he had the heavy build to match. He sat with his arms rested on the table, on one wrist was a huge and complicated looking watch, on the other a heavy gold bracelet. His hair was close cropped, there were tattoos on his fingers and his overall appearance was more than a little threatening. He looked like a man that had never failed to get his own way. He stared at Short for a moment and ignored his question.

"You're not at all difficult to find, you know," he said, "and you owe us money, £20,000 if I'm not mistaken, but the interest is mounting up. And it's all due in a few week's time now. But you must know that." Short did indeed know that, he had been rash in taking out a loan to feed his gambling addiction and had not been careful about its source; not careful at all. He struggled for something to say and summoned up just a few words.

"I'm working on it; I'll get the money." He knew as he said it that it did not sound the least bit convincing.

"Well, that's as maybe, but let's be very clear about what happens if you don't get it shall we – I reckon you'd be looking at a long period of sick leave, right?"

"You can't threaten me like that, I'm a policeman." Short was not sure where that took him but felt he had to say something defensive. It made no difference.

"Not a very bright one evidently, and you don't look like a policeman at the moment, do you? As I said you are not difficult to find. You better get out there and do something to raise the cash. See you in a few days."

The man got up, his bulk then even more evident as he stood, he had taken very few sips of his coffee and now picked up the glass. He looked down on Short for a moment then sloshed the coffee across the table and into his lap and walked away without another word. Short pushed his seat back with a violent jerk, making other customers look up at the noise, and dabbed at himself somewhat ineffectively with a napkin, an action that still left a damp patch across his front. He was fortunate that the coffee had cooled a little and did no real damage. Nevertheless the action made him feel more than a little vulnerable; he put his head in his hands and wondered what on earth he could do. He had just the one idea and wondered if it would prove possible and also if it could produce results in the time he had left.

Chapter Seventeen

Very odd indeed

Left alone Marty turned his mind to what his wife always called his little expeditions and the fact that he had realised that if anything happened to him, either a long stretch in prison which was what he feared Inspector Green had in mind for him, or still worse his untimely demise, there were certain loose ends that needed addressing. He reckoned Tracy was well able to go on running the shop and trusted Mary to work out an arrangement between them, they had already discussed that in normal times. He had finished work on the old Jowett and was proud of its current state, even though it was the car that had helped land him in this mess, it was in a fine saleable state now and, while he liked to think that he was the best to do a deal on it, either Tracy or Mary could no doubt sell it on.

But there was something else that concerned him; he reached for the paper the nurse Beth had got for him, laid it out on the tray table that was set across the bed in front of him and started to write. He had to be very careful what he put, he knew that, and he had made several false starts, crumpling the sheets and throwing them in a bin by his bed. In the end he settled for a few brief phrases and was satisfied with that. He wrote Tracy's name on the envelope, folded the paper and put it inside. He found he was dozy again and let his eyes droop closed.

Later that day as Tracy had got back from a call out – everything occurring in Marty's absence had been routine so far and she felt she had coped well – she saw someone was trying the shop door.

"It's shut up, but I'm here now," she said. "Give me a moment." She produced the keys and opened the door, taking in the figure of a young man perhaps in his mid-twenties and, she allowed herself to think, rather good looking. Tall and fit, with an untidy mop of rather curly brown hair, he had all the characteristics necessary to spark her interest. The on-off relationship she had had for a while was off for good now, it had been for a couple of months, so she found herself noticing such things. She collected her thoughts as she ducked behind the counter, lifting the kind of counter flap made famous by Del Trotter's tumble in the television comedy "Only Fools and Horses", and settling herself on her stool.

"Right, now how can I help you?" He looked at her, paused, and seemed to be struggling to know just what to say.

"I'm James Boon, Jim, I have a stall just over there." His flapped his arm in a rather imprecise way over his shoulder as he tried to indicate its location, before continuing: "You must know the market is rife with rumours about your boss, about Marty, he's a popular figure here, goes back way before my time. No one thinks he's a murderer, but now he's sick and, well, nobody really knows what's happening." He paused again and gave her a slight smile, one that seemed to be as much to encourage himself as her. "Everyone's talking about him, but I wondered about you… are you coping with everything? And, and… I wondered if there was anything I could do to help." She said nothing and after a moment he added: "Is there?" Tracy saw what was going on in an instant, she thought for a brief moment more, and then said outright:

"Are you asking me to go on a date?" A question to which Jim responded at once.

"Well, yes, I guess I am, but I was serious about the help as well, is there anything I can do?"

"I'm not sure, maybe, it's a bit too soon to know what's going to happen. I'm sure this murder business is a mistake." She meant that nothing helpful came to mind at present, but she also thought it might be nice to have someone to talk things over with, so she added: "What about a drink at the end of the day?" Jim agreed at once, his pleasure plain to see, but he had more to say.

"There is something else, I'm not absolutely sure but I think someone is watching this place. You know how it is, there's a pattern to the market, people walk through, they go to stalls or shops and then move on, but this guy's been... what's the right word? He's been, well, sort of hovering. He was there when I came in. Let me look." He turned and stood at the door looking out.

"Yes, he's still there, see, the guy in the jeans and a black sweatshirt, he's slowly going past that clothes stall but not looking at anything, in fact he keeps looking over here. Anyway he's been in this bit of the market for half an hour and bought nothing. It could be he's up to something." Tracy looked and watched for a few minutes as the man headed away and then back again, his slow pace seemed to indicate that he was aiming to stay in about the same spot. When he paused opposite the shop, she recognised him.

"Stay here," she said to Jim in a loud firm voice as she came out from behind the counter, yanked the door open and went out into the market. After weaving about a dozen paces through the crowd she went right up to him.

"I know you," she jabbed a finger into his chest, "you were guarding Marty Holmes at the hospital, just losing the police uniform isn't going to make you invisible you know. What do you want, *Constable*?" The emphasis on the last word was not flattering. Constable Short was taken aback by her unexpected and up front outburst, which had at once sparked interest in those market workers around them and within earshot. He took a step back but then, put on the spot, he tried to sound authoritative.

"He's a person of interest, that's all." He was now conscious of a circle of people all edging closer around him as Tracy replied.

"Well, there are plenty here who are interested in him in a positive way, and no one thinks he's a killer." Short glanced round as he heard a murmur of agreement amongst those around them that made him decide to cut his losses.

"We'll see." He said and stepped out, putting his plans on hold and walking at speed towards Essex Road. Tracy looked round her.

"Thanks guys." She turned and retraced her steps towards the shop, someone called out "Well done, girl." And there were a few more complimentary murmurs, this time of agreement and support. Jim held the door open for her as she went back into the shop.

"Well, I must say, you sure are a feisty one, I wouldn't want to get on your wrong side. Well done. What do you think he was doing out there?" asked Jim.

"No idea, but it seems odd, he was the policeman on guard duty sat outside Marty's room when I visited him in hospital. He seemed not to be taking any part in things, just a bored guard. Seems a bit odd he's here, he's based out in Loughton after all. And yes, you don't."

"Don't? Don't what?" Jim looked puzzled as Tracy smiled.

"Want to get on my wrong side. Pick me up here at six, okay, I think I need that drink." They exchanged mobile numbers in case the arrangement needed to be changed. Jim grinned at her, said that he would see her later and went back to work. Tracy was getting a pleasant vibe about Jim. Once he had spoken up he seemed confident and she, well, she just liked the look of him, he seemed to be somehow more genuine than some of the chancers who approached her. Early days she thought. She put such thoughts out of her mind and fell back into her normal routine, there were no more call outs, but the shop was busy.

By six o'clock when Jim again appeared at the door she was, as she had said, ready for a drink. Besides the more she thought about the police constable hanging around the shop the more odd it seemed. If she had known anything about the way police work was organised she would have been quite sure that it was very odd indeed.

Chapter Eighteen
Do me a favour

Marty woke on what was his third day in hospital feeling he had taken a step back. He felt rough and when his breakfast arrived and he sat up to tackle that he found he could not eat much at all. It was not just the indifferent hospital food, he just did not have any sort of appetite. He lay back on the bed and, seeing Constable Short back on duty outside the open door, his worry about his situation resurfaced and left him feeling even worse.

The policeman had disappeared for a few minutes while Marty struggled to eat, Inspector Green had given him specific instructions to check on the patient's condition as soon as he came on duty. On enquiring at the nurses' station he learned nothing useful and was told that any assessment could not be made until after the doctor had done his morning round. When he phoned the inspector with his update he had not been pleased, Constable Short was savvy enough not to point out that it was not his fault, but the inspector's tone somehow made him feel it was. He was told to phone again when there was any news and had returned to his boring vigil. The inspector still saw Marty as the route to a quick, and impressive, conviction and was not about to give up on that prospect, he planned to speak to Marty again as soon as he was discharged.

"Morning Marty, how are you today?" He looked up to find it was Beth checking up on him. Marty was noncommittal.

"Oh, you know, I just want to get out of here." He glanced beyond her at the policeman and added: "And as far away from him as possible."

"I'm sure you do, let's see what the doctor says. It's early yet, but once he's seen you we'll know better. I think there's a good chance you'll be going home today. Anything I can get you?" Marty declined.

"No, thanks, you're very kind." Then he had a thought, one he felt would make sure of things.

"Actually yes, if anything happens to me can you do me a bit of a favour and pass on a message to Tracy? You know, the young woman who came in with my wife soon after I got here, she works in the shop with me."

"Now there's no need for you to talk like that, I'm sure you will be out of here soon, but yes, of course I can. But I think you had a phone with you when you came in, it will be in your locker, do you want that? We can charge it up if necessary and you could give her a call?" Marty did not want to explain, he couldn't, so settled for a simple request.

"Thanks, but this is only for if something happens to me, you know. It may well sound odd, I know, but just tell her to look under my favourite thing. Just that, she'll figure it out. Tell her that too, the figuring it out bit that is. Okay?" Beth smiled at him and repeated it back.

"Alright. Of course, but don't you worry, I'm sure you can tell her yourself soon enough. Now, take it easy. You should see the doctor in an hour or so." Given the somewhat ambiguous nature of the message, Beth grabbed a sheet of paper from his tray table and made a note, which she folded and put in her pocket. Beth was not so often asked to run that sort of errand, and she did not know the exact meaning of Marty's rather ambiguous words, but she was concerned to look after her patients in every way possible. Once outside the room, she went to her locker and stuck the note to the inside of the door as a reminder. Once she had left the room Marty relaxed and dozed.

Soon after Marty had finished his conversation with Beth, Tracy arrived in Chapel Market to open up the shop. Although she was there on time a customer was already waiting outside the door.

"Morning, you after me?" She addressed the man as she unlocked the door. "Come in, give me a moment to get organised, how can I help?" The man fumbled in his pocket, pulled out a handful of change and extracted a key from it, which he then handed over to Tracy.

"I wonder, can you do me a duplicate of this key?" he asked. Tracy took the key from him and looked at it.

"Just a sec, I need to check." She stepped through to the stock room, removed a manufacture's catalogue from a shelf above the desk and returned with it to the counter. After thumbing through it she delivered her verdict.

"It's not a very common kind this, I can't just cut you a duplicate, but I can order you one, should have it in a couple of days. Will that be okay?" The man asked the price and she told him the figure. There followed a bit of to and fro because she asked for payment up front, she explained that if he never returned to the shop again the key was no use to her and the money spent would be a lost. He hesitated, but in the end seemed to understand the situation and paid up; she wrote out a receipt for him and handed it over. Tracy did not want Marty coming back to find that she had wasted money. She took the customer's number and promised to phone when the key had been delivered.

That done she thought back to the previous evening, Jim had appeared on the dot of six and they had gone first to her regular haunt of the greasy spoon café for a cup of tea and a donut, which she called lunch as it had been a hectic day. Safety in numbers she reckoned, there would be people in the café she knew and if their meeting was a disaster and she wanted to duck out before long she could do so without hassle. But the reverse was true, she and Jim got on well. It was no surprise that the subject of Marty came up, and Tracy explained that the police suspected him of killing George Godwin, though she did not go into any detail, after all it was still unclear how things would play out and his health was the most immediate and important concern; she just said they all had to be patient.

"He's not under arrest, he had a stroke before they had got to that stage, and he's still in hospital. Mary, that's his wife, will update me when she knows anything more. It's all nonsense of course, Marty couldn't hurt a fly as they say. I'm sure it will all blow over. He's been very good to me." She began to tell Jim something of her journey from cardboard boxes to locks, and then suggested they move on.

"Come on, you promised me a proper drink. What we need is a pub. Any ideas?" Jim suggested a walk along the canal and they walked through the market, across Essex Road and onwards. They then spent several hours in "The Island Queen", a well-known traditional pub that was something of an institution in the area and was tucked away in the side streets of Islington close by the canal. They had a couple of drinks, then decided to get something to eat and ordered fish and chips and, as Tracy told her mother later, "we just talked and talked". It all seemed to bode well and they went their separate ways with Tracy agreeing to Jim's suggestion to meet again and adding persistence to the list of characteristics she was laying against him.

Back in the hospital the doctor's regular morning round was late, an all too often occurrence in light of the volatile nature of the ward's affairs, this time urgent admissions had meant a good deal of switching around to make sure sufficient beds were free. Beth found herself reassuring several anxious patients, telling each that "the doctor will be round to see you soon". As she said this to one patient she thought of Marty tucked away in a side room, she knew that he could not see or hear much of what was going on in the ward so she went to speak to him. The constable at his door was engrossed in doing something on his phone and did not look up.

As she entered the room she thought Marty was asleep but, almost at once, something about him and his ashen face warned her that was not the case. She approached the bed, fearing the worst as she checked further, and one close up look had her pressing a red emergency button set above the bedhead before she rushed back to the door.

"I need some help in here. Now." She repeated the phrase in a shout and as she did so Constable Short stepped into the room, she turned back to find him standing by the bed.

"What goes on?" He asked.

"Out of here now, you - I think he's had another stroke." The constable retreated and the next few minutes saw a flurry of activity in the room as the doctor and another nurse joined Beth at Marty's bedside. The doctor's examination did not last long however as he established at once what had happened; his conclusion was then inevitable.

"I'm afraid he's had another stroke, and a little while ago by the looks of it. There's nothing we can do now, sadly he's gone." Although those working in hospitals get used to such things happening, they are not unaffected by it, Beth had begun to rather like Marty and she felt, not for the first time, that life was unfair.

"Are you sure?" Beth asked the doctor, allowing no pause for an answer and adding: "Sorry, silly question, but last time I saw him he seemed to be doing okay."

"Yes. I did think I would be discharging him this morning, however strokes are often inclined to be unpredictable, I'm afraid. If it's any comfort I don't think he would have known anything about it." Beth felt a tear form in her eye, she turned away and dabbed at it with a tissue.

"Thank you everyone." The doctor was not unsympathetic, but now adopted a business like tone. "You know what to do next." He stated a time of death to be recorded on Marty's notes. Procedure then soon set in and, not least someone would have to inform Marty's wife. Beth left the room to get things organised, as she went out she snapped at the constable.

"Right, you heard the situation, I think I'd like you out of here now, please." Left alone outside a room now empty expect for Marty's body lying in the bed Constable Short stepped back inside the room. He looked at Marty's motionless figure and his first thought was unfeeling and selfish: that he was off the hook - no more tedious hospital guard duty. As he reached for his phone to inform the inspector of what had occurred he noticed the envelope lying on the tray table, he glanced at the name on it, picked it up and put it in his pocket. Once he had reported in he left the hospital and the note went with him, maybe he thought, given what he now knew about Marty, it was something that might help him.

Chapter Nineteen

The only thing that mattered

After he had passed on the news of Marty's death to Inspector Green, Constable Short knew he would have no more to do with the case, if indeed there was anything else to be done. But he did have the note he had stolen that Marty had written to Tracy and hoped that might help him. He had heard enough of the unfolding situation to share the inspector's view that Marty was a crook, in all likelihood a thief of some long standing if he had had enough confidence to tackle a villain with George Godwin's nasty reputation. The constable reckoned that where there was a villain, a thief, there would in all probability to be the fruits of his endeavours or at least that from his most recent exploits, hidden somewhere, perhaps somewhere he could locate. He thought it might just provide a solution to his financial woes.

Later in a quiet moment he opened the note and read it. It was very brief, but even so a full half of the page was covered by Marty's large sprawling handwriting. It said:

Tracy. If anything happens to me I know I can rely on you to look after the shop. Mary will work out financial details with you. Just talk to her. And please do something else – look under my favourite thing, right – and figure it out. You'll do well, with the shop, I know you will. Holmes and Hines remember. Take care.

Underneath was Marty's name. His writing made it take up about a quarter of the page. Short did not think the message was much help, but resolved to find out more, thinking doing so might mean resorting to some more drastic action. He knew the clock was ticking on his financial problem.

Inspector Green received the news of Marty's death with a feeling that blended huge disappointment with anger. So much so that when Constable Short had telephoned him he had his head bitten off just for breaking the news. The inspector had thought the prompt solving of the killing of a man such as Godwin was going to be a useful stepping stone on his route to becoming Chief Inspector, now, although he would still record it as a success – a death explained and laid at someone's door as far as the file went – it would not weigh much in the balance of his achievements. He had taken the call about the death in his office and, as he sat regretting the path events had taken, there was a knock at the door. It was Sergeant James who arrived with a question. He had not heard the news.

"Morning Sir, any news about the Godwin case, what's next on the agenda?" Inspector Green gritted his teeth as he explained that the case was now over.

"Marty Holmes is dead. Had another stroke it seems, perhaps that's justice for you. Anyway now we'll probably never know the details of what happened that night but there's no doubt that they were together in the house when Godwin got shot. My money would still be on it being murder, but... anyway, it's done, case closed. See to the paperwork, will you, and file it away." The inspector just wanted to forget the whole thing, he had just got details of a stabbing that had taken place during a raid on a jewellery shop; he reckoned that could be a useful one for him too. The sergeant promised to do just that, Green's attitude to the thing had made it a difficult case and he too could not wait to forget all about it. He hoped whatever they found themselves working on next would both prove easier and not get the inspector so wound up.

Mary Holmes reaction was, of course, very different. She heard the news by telephone from the hospital. It was the kind of call that sadly had to be made on such occasions and so, in some respects such a call was routine, the fact of it might have been routine but the task of making such a call was always difficult and always affecting. No matter what was said and how it was said, and those making such calls always tried as hard as possible to be sensitive, the blunt fact was: someone had died, almost always someone close to the recipient of the phone call.

Nothing that could be said changed the bald fact. And the news, however much it might be expected in some cases, was always going to be a shock to the system, one that would doubtless change so much, and could do so in so many different ways.

In Mary's case it was a profound shock, she knew the possibility existed of course, the doctor had made it clear more than once, but all her hopes and expectations were that Marty would come home, that their life together would go on. After all he had seemed to be making good progress. She had taken the call in the kitchen as she got a cake out of the oven. The call had not lasted very long and had ended with practical matters, an invitation for her to come into the hospital to see to a number of procedural matters. Afterwards she had walked through to the living room and sat down, sitting there for a long time, still and for the moment unaware of the time or her surroundings. After a while, a time she could not even have guessed at, she wiped tears from her eyes, tears of which she was unaware as they had added a silent accompaniment to her last few moments, and with a force of effort made a phone call. She needed someone with her and at a time like this that meant family: she rang her sister Betty. She lived fifty miles north of London in a rural village; she had always hated London, but Mary knew she would come.

They had an awkward conversation, neither quite sure what to say, but Betty, also shocked of course, gave her commiserations and said she would be there later in the day, she would phone when she had sorted a few things out at home and packed a bag; she would stay for a few days. Mary thanked her and thought how difficult every contact like this would be, Marty was only 59 years old and very few people, apart from friends in the market, even knew he was in hospital. People needed to be told. It would be shocks all round. She wondered what to do next; she could not face the hospital so soon. She was about to phone Tracy, after all this affected her too, albeit in a rather different kind of way, then lost her nerve and sent a short text:

Second stroke proved fatal. Talk later.

She knew she should say more, the few words seemed so perfunctory, but she couldn't think how to say more, she couldn't concentrate.

She had a reply from Tracy within a couple of minutes; it was even shorter, consisting of a single word:
Coming.

Tracy must have shut up the shop and hurried straight over because it was a matter of a few minutes before the doorbell rang. In the past Mary and Tracy had never been on hugging terms, Tracy had seen Mary a good deal during the last year, sometimes socially and on other occasions when shop business needed discussing with Marty and Mary together, now though Mary found herself standing in her hall in a protracted hug, one which Tracy came straight through the door and initiated. She spoke as they broke apart.

"I'm so, so sorry, I can't believe it... I really don't know what to say, but you know I will do anything I can to help." Tracy made tea, telling Mary it was the mandatory reaction for the English in such circumstances. After a further awkwardness when neither knew what to say to the other and a period when Mary just sobbed, they both found themselves babbling. Tracy reiterated her sympathy; Mary assured her that she should not worry about the shop, her livelihood was guaranteed; Tracy said she shouldn't worry about things like that at the moment.

The reassurance went to and fro until, after a while, Mary succeeded in pulling herself together somewhat.

"My sister Betty will be here later in the day, she lives just outside London, she'll stay for a little while. So I won't be on my own. But the hospital want me to visit, there are... well, things to be done and I'd like to get that over before Betty arrives. Would you come with me do you think?" Tracy agreed at once and they set off in Mary's car with Mary insisting she was okay to drive.

"Marty had the van and his old bangers of course, but the bangers were not drivable most of the time, this was our car, but it was always referred to as mine." That did not matter of course, it was of no consequence, nor was anything else they spoke of on the way to the hospital. The one thing that mattered was something neither of them wanted nor knew quite how to speak about: Marty.

Once at Whipps Cross the hospital 'procedures', as they had been referred to on the phone, did not take too long and were dealt with in a way that tried to combine sympathy with efficiency, nevertheless they were there the best part of two hours, most of that time spent waiting and being passed around from one person to another. The doctor who had looked after Marty and who Mary had met on her visits spoke to them, he was sympathetic but also made it clear that 'it was just one of those things', that 'it's an unfortunate fact that life isn't fair' and that 'there was no one to blame and nothing to be angry about'. He assured her that Marty would have felt no pain. Mary knew he was right: the main task for her now was to concentrate on the things that needed to be done, she was going to be busy: a funeral to arranged, the shop to reorganise, finances and a will to be dealt with and more, much more. But she also had to cope with the fact that Marty was not there anymore, there was a huge hole in her life and it was one that could not be got over in a moment. She found the full implications of that were only just beginning to dawn on her. Just before they left Mary got a call from her sister to say that she was on her way.

With matters settled at the hospital, and documentation issued that would allow the death to be registered, they drove back to Mary's house. Inside Tracy made more tea and insisted Mary eat something. She rummaged in the fridge and made sandwiches for them, thinking that there should be something more substantial she could do, but even this much seemed to help and when Mary's sister Betty arrived a little while later she found them in the kitchen preparing yet more tea to go with the cake Mary had baked just before she got the news. Tracy was introduced, but allowed Betty to take over and took her leave without getting involved in their conversation. She hoped Mary would be better for having Betty there.

"I'm so very sorry Mary, I wish there was more I could do, but family is best, I'm sure Betty will support you. I'll keep the shop going, don't worry about that and let me know if I can help in any other way. Do you want me to tell people around the market? Just telling one will see everyone knowing almost at once. You know how it goes." Mary agreed that she could begin to spread the word and Tracy bade them goodbye. She felt for Mary, of course she did, but she also couldn't help but wonder what Marty's death meant for her and her job. She could imagine scenarios that would be difficult for her; maybe Mary would want or need to sell the shop. She reckoned anything like that was some way off though and went through the market to find Jim, if she told him and one or two others the news that would be job done.

Chapter Twenty

He was a good man

Betty did not look as if she was Mary's sibling. She was just a few years younger, a couple of stone heavier and a foot taller than her sister and, in part because she had moved out of London once she had left school, she had experienced a rather different life. She had married a solicitor and they had two children, both now at university; this too separated her a little from her sister as Mary had no family. Nevertheless the two siblings had always got on well and, although they did not see each other every five minutes, they kept in touch and had always met up on a regular basis over the years. It had been impractical for her to drive into town, parking would be a real problem, one made worse as she intended to stay for a while, so she had caught a train to Liverpool Street Station and got a taxi to Mary's home.

When Mary opened the door neither said a word until after she had stepped inside, and a lengthy hug had taken place.

Betty's first words acknowledged the awkwardness of the situation.

"I'm so sorry," she said, "this is so sad, poor you, I really don't know what to say, it was all so sudden, one minute he was in hospital, then he seemed to be getting better, then he was gone. I can still not believe it. It seems impossible." Mary thanked her for coming, and they paused while Tracy took her leave. Mary felt there was no need to go into the details about what had happened as they had already spoken on the phone a number of times since Marty went into hospital. However, Mary had not told her about Marty's brush with the law, indeed Betty knew nothing of Marty's extra-curricular activities. Mary had thought about this and decided that, as people were certain to be speaking about this at the funeral, she had to say something. But she resolved not to go into any detail, besides she had heard nothing further from the police in Loughton and was beginning to assume that was the end of the unfortunate matter as far as she was concerned.

"There's something you should know Betty, Marty was being questioned by the police when he had the first stroke and was taken to hospital. He had been with someone when they died and the police suspected he might have had something to do with it. He didn't of course, Marty would never hurt a fly, you know that, and he was never charged. I am sure it would all just have gone away, but anyway, now he is... now he has passed away, the police seem to have dropped it all." Betty was itching to interrupt her but, seeing this, Mary held up a hand and insisted that she finished her little speech. "It was just a misunderstanding and was one that only occurred because he was alone with the other man at the time. I really don't want to talk about it now – there's too much else to cope with. But I thought you might hear it mentioned at the funeral so I had to say something." She stopped and Betty could see that the matter was to be set on one side for the moment whatever she might do or say. So she changed the subject.

"You know I always liked Marty, and I'm sure you're right about him. Right, put that kettle of yours on again, we'll have a cuppa and make a list of what must be done. I'm here to help, remember, and you've got a funeral to organise, well, we have that is." They sat together drinking tea, Mary just grateful not to be on her own, and began to make a list. Some of what needed to be done was just procedural – Betty organised the registration of death – and between them they mentioned things such as freezing bank accounts. But they talked for a long while about the funeral, something Mary was quick to admit she and Marty had never spoken about in any real detail, although his will was specific: he was to be cremated. Betty cleared away the tea things, got some supper organised, telling Mary that she had to eat to keep her strength up, and then she took the lead as they began to get things organised.

"You know you said that something eco-friendly would be good," said Betty as they discussed the details of the funeral. "Well, look what I've found online." She held out her phone for Mary to see. "Creative Coffins it's called, cardboard is the main material, economical and eco-friendly to boot. And, best of all, they all have jazzy designs on them – this one features a classic car. How about that?" The following morning they had taken the death certificate Mary had obtained from the hospital and used it to initiate the formal registering of Marty's death, selected and visited a funeral director and decided how to organise things. Mary explained to them that Marty had left instructions that he was to be cremated to avoid the drama of a coffin being lowered into the ground in what he had said was most likely to be in drab surroundings and pouring rain. She said they had talked about that a while back. The nearest crematorium was a bit of a way off in Finchley.

"Most of our friends are local," Mary told Betty back at the house, "and they all work, many, as you know, in the market. I think we should have as minimal a service as possible at the crem and then have a get together in a local pub in the evening. I want to celebrate Marty's life more than anything; people will like that and, if that gathering is in the evening then more people will be able to come without disrupting their work.

"Sounds like the best idea," agreed Betty. "So which pub suits?" Mary mentioned several, but they settled on 'The Earl of Essex' on the basis that Mary reckoned they could do a deal there to have exclusive use of the place for an evening.

"Come on then, I'll buy you a drink and we'll check out that pub," said Betty a day or two later as evening approached. Betty was doing a good job of jollying Mary along, keeping her busy and getting everything sorted, though their time together was punctuated by tearful moments. They returned from the pub later with a satisfactory arrangement made and began to work out who now needed to be informed and how that would be done.

On the day all went well, despite the prospect of the evening at the pub, which could be taken to mean attending was not necessary, a good few people came to the short service at the crematorium in the morning where, a simple ceremony concluded what Mary saw as the worst stage of the proceedings. Tracy shut the shop and she and Jim joined the people attending; she was pleased when Jim had insisted he must go with her. She found she became quite tearful and was grateful to be able to hold Jim's hand. There were no flowers, Mary had requested that instead people who wanted should make a donation to charity; she specified Headway, an organisation that focused on strokes. Flowers may therefore have been limited to a solitary wreath from Mary, but the colourful 'classic car' coffin drew many a smile and was judged by all to be a good idea. Betty's husband had joined them for the day, and both the children, Mary's nephew and niece, had travelled from university to be there. Betty stuck to Mary like glue throughout the service, there were tears, of course, but soon they were back at the house for the traditional reviving cup of tea and the sandwiches which Betty had made first thing and which gave them a simple lunch. The two sisters expressed the view that it was good to have that stage over and anticipated the evening being a much easier experience.

And so it was. A good crowd assembled and Mary felt she had to welcome them and say something, despite doing that sort of thing not being her forte and others offering to speak for her. The landlord of the pub provided a crate for her to stand on and rang his 'time gentlemen please' bell to ensure silence. It took Mary a moment to get going, she had a firm grip with one hand on a note she had made to guide her but managed to speak up well.

"Thank you all for coming, it's a great comfort to see so many friends here. I'll be brief: Marty has gone and gone suddenly, unexpectedly and in difficult circumstances as most of you know. But he was a good man, and a good husband – we had been very happy together for more than thirty years – he may have had his faults, we all do, and I never found a way of getting him to shut up about those wretched old bangers of his, but he was a good man and… for the record, he wouldn't hurt a fly. You can be absolutely sure that certain recent rumours about him were not true. Enough of that. He was, I believe, well liked and well respected locally and… and, I'll miss him more than I can say." Tracy found listening to Mary speak made her quite emotional, she was very conscious that Marty had been so very good to her, working with him had changed her life in a radical and positive way, besides she had got to like him too. She felt a tear in her eye and clung to Jim as Mary finished speaking and Betty hastened forward extending a hand to help her climb down off the crate. They were not in church, nor even in the crematorium, so people felt free to follow their instinctive reactions, and the considerable applause that followed was interspersed with many a "Hear, hear". Next someone proposed a toast and Marty's name rippled round the room as that was enacted with enthusiasm, tables were thumped, and glasses raised high.

Despite the inevitable awkwardness of such an occasion, a good evening was had by all after Mary had spoken and she had a long parade of people coming up to her to pay their respects and agree with her assessment of Marty. Betty stayed close and helped her over a number of difficult moments and later, once they were back home, they both agreed that it had been a good and suitable send off. It was also the end of an era and Mary would need to get used to a rather different way of life in future. First, there were still some matters to be sorted.

Chapter Twenty-One

So it's a deal

Constable Short was not in a good mood, he had returned a number of times to the note stolen from Marty and intended for Tracy, which he had now had in his possession for more than a couple of weeks, and he still couldn't work out what it meant or see any way in which it could help him get his hands on the spoils he very much believed Marty Holmes had left hidden somewhere. He was sure there might well be some though, and he was resolved to have a damn good go at getting his hands on anything there was. He did not propose to give up and had come to the conclusion that some more direct intervention might be the way because time was running out and he still had no other way of finding the money he needed to repay his debt.

He was not on duty and not therefore in uniform, but with his warrant card as always in his wallet, he set off for Holmes & Son in Chapel Market.

Things had settled down somewhat for Tracy. The funeral was past and she and Mary had spoken about the shop and how it would be run in future. She had reckoned it was too soon for such a conversation, Mary was still grieving, but Mary had insisted, saying that Marty would have 'wanted things put straight without delay' and explaining again that she found it a great deal easier to cope when she was busy with things to do. There were some details to work out still but Tracy reckoned it was too soon to bother Mary further with that at present. Things were fine as they were she reckoned, though on one point she had decided to take some action.

She had experienced a good year working under a skilled tutor, but she realised that she still had things to learn, a good many things if she was ever to be as good as her mentor. Yet it was a practical business she was now in and there was a good deal she could not learn by reading a book or checking something out on Google or You Tube. Since she had been running the shop on her own most things had gone well, though she had been asked to do a number of jobs which were beyond her current skills. Refusing them, thus turning business away, did not give her a good feeling, in large part because the more complex work was often amongst the most profitable too. It worried her for a while, she wanted the new arrangement with Mary to work well, but this was something of a handicap; then she had an idea.

Marty had a friend, Steve Jessop, he was someone who she had met a number of times over the last year or so. He had a similar business, a shop down beyond Liverpool Street Station in Aldgate. They had exchanged a few words at Marty's funeral and he had told her that if she ever needed any help she was to let him know. She rang him and asked if they could get together so that she could bend his ear about something. He agreed at once without asking what it was about and she arranged to meet him at his shop at closing time the following day.

She arrived at Steve's shop to find that the sign on the door read "Closed" but that the door was unlocked. Opening it she stepped in and, there being no sign of Steve, she called out.

"Hello, Steve. Anyone there?" Steve appeared at once from the back premises, the shop layout was not unlike that at Holmes & Son, and smiled at her.

"Hello to you Tracy," he said. "Welcome. More to the point, what can I do for you?"

"I've got a proposition for you Steve, is there somewhere nearby we can go and get a cuppa? I'll buy."

"Sure." Steve agreed to go with her and once outside he locked up and led the way to a café round the corner, a place not unlike Marty's favourite haunt in the market. Steve found them a table and, true to her word, Tracy went to the counter and ordered and paid for two teas, which she was told would be delivered to the table. Almost before she was back to her seat a waitress followed her back and delivered two steaming mugs.

"Okay, now what's all this about? Hang on a minute, let me ask you this first: how's Mary doing? Poor woman, it was all so sudden," said Steve and Tracy brought him up to date.

"Well she's upset of course, devastated, but the funeral went well I think, so she has that behind her and can regard it as a success, I think. I'm looking after the shop and Marty's affairs were not too complicated, so I think she's getting everything sorted, albeit one step at a time. I know she misses him terribly, they'd been married such a long time. At least she must have lots of good memories."

"I'm sure she's upset, these things are never easy, but she's a strong woman that one, has there been..." Steve paused for a moment, wondering whether to raise the issue or not, then he went on: "err, has there been any further word from the police?" This was a sore point.

"Everyone who knew him is quite sure he didn't murder that Godwin character; much more likely it was an accident or self-defence. I bet he would never have gone there if he had known Godwin was around." Tracy had not quoted any of the details she had heard in the hospital when Marty told Mary what had happened to anyone. Least said the better she reckoned and Mary had agreed. She went on: "Anyway there's not been another word from the police, well there's no way they can charge him with anything now is there? And George Godwin's dead and buried; good riddance I say, there's no more to be done there. So it looks like the file's been closed as they say. It would be better to have Marty cleared, as it were, but he was there in the house after all, so case dropped is as good as we'll get, I think. Anyway, he was never charged with anything."

"Sly old dog though, eh, but I'm sure you're right about murder, there is no way Marty would ever have done anything like that. It's all a sad business though and no mistake." They both sat in silence for some moments sipping tea, Marty's death weighing on them both in different ways. Then Tracy put down her mug and pitched in.

"Right, let's get to it, here's my idea. I'm doing alright at the shop, I cope with most of the work but I still have a lot of stuff to learn, right, and I'm getting some enquiries I have to turn down 'cos I either just can't do the work or might struggle with the technicalities of it somewhat. At the moment, that is. So here's what I thought - I *do* take on those things in future but I sub-contract them to you... with one condition." Steve didn't actually raise an eyebrow, but his look was quizzical.

"Which is what exactly?"

"That we go to the job together and you tutor me, show me what's what, so that I can expand my range of work. You can keep the money those jobs pay and as my patch so to speak is not so far away it would be convenient extra business for you – for a while at least. I'm a fast learner! So, what do you think, would that work?" Tracy smiled to herself at her last remark, she had no intention of giving good business away for very long. Then her face turned serious as she saw Steve was giving the idea some real thought.

"Well, yes, I don't see why not, Marty was a good sort, well apart from the thieving evidently, but we were good mates too and I'd like to help. Besides, you're right, it would be extra business for me, I would even be prepared to work labelled as a

Holmes & Son person so that any repeat business comes back to you. It seems a useful and practical arrangement for us both."

"That's great. So it's a deal." Tracy stuck out her hand and Steve held it rather than shook it, taking his time before releasing it as she added: "By the way the shop's name's going to be Holmes & Hines in future, the shop front is to be repainted, we're keeping Marty's name, of course, not least because Mary's still involved." They chatted on for a while, Tracy mentioning the kind of job she envisaged their arrangement would involve until, drinks finished, and deal done, she excused herself.

"Must get back," she said, "I want to tell Mary about this and Jim too, he's been very supportive."

"Ah yes, Jim the boyfriend, now I remember him from the funeral. Okay."

"Just thought I'd mention Jim, after that lengthy handshake and all. Besides you're old enough to be my father!" They grinned at each other and parted on good terms, with Tracy congratulating herself on what she believed would be a useful arrangement for herself and Steve and promising Steve that she would be in touch as and when suitable jobs came along. She set off getting a bus towards Islington and looking forward to telling Jim that the suggestion she had told him about was all set up and agreed. It was early days with Jim she knew, but they had been seeing a good deal of each other and she had a good feeling about him. He had been great during the past few weeks when, after all, Marty's death had thrown her life into some degree of turmoil. She reckoned that sexy and supportive was a pretty good combination.

Having just dismissed the police as being out of the picture when she spoke to Steve, Tracy was not to know that the following day would bring another encounter her way and an unwelcome one at that.

Chapter Twenty-Two

We'll say nothing

At the end of the following day Tracy had not yet closed the shop but was sitting at Marty's desk faced with an untidy pile of paper. It would be a while before she thought of that desk in any other way than as being Marty's. Working the shop on her own she had soon realised that running a small business involved a good many things beyond the actual locksmith work, and that paperwork was just one of those things; if she did not do it then it would not get done at all and, with all that had gone on in the last week or two, she had let matters mount up somewhat. Marty had never done that, 'little and often' he had always said, and she could now see that was a pretty good philosophy; it was one that did indeed make things easier. She planned to keep on top of the paperwork from now on, and reckoned that would make it easier to cope with even if some discipline was necessarily involved in doing so. She punched holes in the sheet she was holding and filed it away in a ring arch file.

Her attention was drawn away from the desk as the shop bell rang. She got up and went to the counter to be faced with the figure of Constable Short, dressed not in uniform but in jeans and a sweatshirt. He held out his warrant card for inspection.

"Yeah, I know who are. What do you want? Marty's gone, you know that, there's nothing you can pin on him now. Why don't you leave us alone?"

"Yes, and George Godwin is gone too, probably a good thing that. But the evidence was clear: it showed that Marty was there in the house and I don't think he went there to kill Godwin, I don't know exactly how that happened, but I reckon he went there to steal, goodness knows what that man had tucked away. What's more I think there's a very good chance whatever he took from Godwin is here in this shop." He noted Tracy's puzzled expression and added: "Whether you know it or not. What say we have a look?"

"You have no right to do that, you need a warrant. I thought you were no more than a low level guard dog. This isn't even your patch. I want you to leave. Get out." Tracy found a defensive instinct cut in and she reacted with a harsh tone, but Short turned, reversed the door sign to "Closed" and clicked the lock to prevent any interruption.

"But I'm the police, you know that, you saw the warrant card, you don't want to hinder a police inquiry now do you?" His tone was unpleasant, and Tracy's anger increased.

"I certainly want to hinder you. Get out, I'm sure you need a warrant to search somewhere." He again ignored her reference to search warrants, raised the hatch in the counter and started to come through. Tracy stepped sideways to block him and without any warning he hit her: a slap, a hard slap across the face. It made Tracy gasp out loud, she stumbled back, putting a hand to her face and clutching at the counter top to steady herself. She was as much surprised as hurt. He ignored her and pushed past into the stock room.

"Let's see, maybe you know where he hid his stuff. Do you?" At this point Tracy, still stunned by his action and with a hand held to her smarting face, realised this was not any sort of police inquiry, it was a rogue policeman trying it on. She also realised she needed help.

"I've no idea what you're talking about. If Marty had secrets he didn't share them with me." As she spoke she slipped her phone out, checked Short was not looking, and, fingers moving at a pace, sent a text Jim: she wrote one single word: "Help". She just prayed he was still nearby, he should be busy closing up his stall. As Short stood in the stockroom looking round for any potential hiding places she spoke again, this time aiming to keep him talking and perhaps slow down anything else he might do before Jim arrived. She prayed he was on his way.

"This is just you isn't it, it's nothing to do with the police - what will that inspector of yours make of what you're doing here?"

"I'm sure you won't say anything to him, just give him ideas that would – he'd be instigating a search here in a moment. And I'd be praised for my initiative. Besides who do you think he'd believe - you or me?" Tracy had little doubt about that and watched as he pulled open the desk drawers one at a time each one revealing a series of untidy interiors stuffed with papers and bits and pieces of the trade: keys, padlocks and more. It was a state she had more than once resolved to tidy up.

"Where's the safe?" He asked, turning towards her in what seemed to be a menacing way that made her think he might hit her again.

"There's not a safe here, people tend not to try and rob locksmiths, have you seen the lock on the door? It's state of the art."

"I don't believe you I..." He was interrupted by the noise of Jim pounding on the shop door. He continued knocking and shouted too, his voice clear within the shop and rising way above any noise in the market.

"What's going on in there? Tracy, open the door, are you okay?" As this went on within a few seconds several people appeared alongside and around him, all curious at his outburst and ready to help if needed. Tracy and Short stood unmoving staring at each other for a long moment.

"You going on with this in front of witnesses?" She glanced across at the door. "Lots of witnesses." Judging that he had been forced to reconsider his position, she pushed past him and hurried towards the door, unlocked it, swung it open and stepped out. As Jim reached for her she found Short had followed in her footsteps and stepped out behind her.

"Police business. There's nothing to see here." He waved his card as he spoke then strode away at speed and disappeared in the crowd. Tracy gave a sigh of relief and she and Jim hugged and went into the shop.

"Are you okay? What happened?" He ran a finger down her cheek, which he at once saw was an unnatural red colour. "Did he hit you?" Tracy turned and locked the door.

"Let's get away from here and I'll tell you all about it," she said. They stepped out into the market again, she locked the door and headed straight off towards the café as she added: "I think some tea is in order." She remembered as they walked that tea had been Marty's solution to every kind of problem. She could hear him saying: "Let's have a cuppa and think about it, eh?" She smiled to herself at the thought. A few minutes on found them sitting in the café, both with mugs of tea and a KitKat; Jim had insisted she needed a sugar boost. She described to him what had happened.

"So, he's after Marty's ill-gotten gains and it's him doing it not any sort of follow up police investigation, is that right?" Jim posed it as a question and Tracy nodded; he went on: "I think you're right: no search warrant and his hitting you like that rather proves the point doesn't it? How's your face feeling now?" Tracy was holding a cloth wrapping a number of ice cubes to the side of her face; it was something rustled up by the café owner when they'd ordered at the counter. She lowered it.

"Yes, getting better, I think, but it bloody well stung. What a bastard."

"I'm sure it did, come on, we need to report him, we should take a photo of your face too, before the red fades. I'll come with you to the police station." Tracy shook her head, found it hurt to do so, and raised the ice pack to her cheek again.

"No. No, we can't do that, listen, don't you see? He's right, it would just open up a whole new area of interest for the police. That Inspector Green would want to search for anything Marty might have hidden away and what if there *is* stuff like that somewhere? It's the last thing Mary would want too, worst of all now while she's grieving." They sat for a moment without speaking as Jim took in what she said and realised she could well be right.

"Alright, we'll say nothing, at least if nothing more happens. But if this turns into a vendetta and Constable Whatsh's-name comes back, I am not having you in danger again - promise me you'll think again. Yes?" Tracy agreed, reminded him that they had promised themselves a trip to the cinema that evening and said they should forget about Short, after all he had found nothing and indeed she was pretty sure that there was nothing to find. But unknown to her, although Short had found nothing tangible, he had learnt something. And it was a particular something that he felt might well help his search in a big way.

Chapter Twenty-Three

He was onto something

A few days later Constable Short paid Tracy another visit. He thought he had managed to walk through the market without being recognised, but almost as soon as he had entered the shop, a head had poked round the door: he had been spotted by another of the market stall holders around at the time of his previous visit. The market had a close knit element to it and there was a strong tendency for people to help each other, there were also a good few people working there that had no good words to say about the police. Both factors had a bearing here. As Tracy looked up from her task, hit a switch and as the grinding noise of the key cutting machine died away, Short had yet to say a single word. The stall holder spoke up first:

"You alright in there Tracy? I thought all that police business was all finished."

"Yes, I'm sure it is. Constable Short is just leaving... Isn't. That. Right?" She glared at the policeman as she spoke, emphasising the last few words so that they posed a question. Short realised that the events of his previous visit now meant that he had little or no chance of being able to get to spend time in the shop without witnesses. He might not be able to get hold of what he had seen on his last visit, but he had information now and he reckoned there were other ways he could proceed. He again decided to cut his losses, turned and left without a word, but his sour look failed to convince Tracy that she had seen the last of him. She thanked her rescuer who did not pursue the matter or ask awkward questions but just returned to his stall.

A while later Short had completed some shopping and he had purchased a hefty pair of bolt cutters. What he had seen in the shop and failed to get hold of was a key. It was one of a number hanging on hooks above the desk in the locksmith's stock room and was attached by a key ring to a plastic tab on which was written the words "Lock up". This was a place he now knew of and had concluded might well be another location it would be worthwhile for him to search. Back at the station he had been able to find out the location of Marty's lock up without any difficulty. No police officer enjoyed the dreaded hospital guard duty and it was judged to be a plausible reason for him wanting to know something about the case that had kept him sitting alone and bored in a hospital corridor for so many hours.

Someone in CID had needed little persuasion to let him have a look at the file.

The lock up was down a quiet alley housing nothing but a number of similar lockups, the one belonging to the locksmith, identified by the faded word Holmes stencilled at the top of one of the doors, being the solitary double one. Short took a look around him and saw no one. He felt in his pocket and pulled out a pair of gloves; he put them on. It then took a matter of moments for him to undo the padlock and that was because the tool he had bought was a good one; it was a modern and heavy duty padlock but it was soon bypassed. He opened the door just wide enough to enter and slipped inside pulling the door to behind him and putting the bolt cutters away in a canvas bag he had arrived with slung over his shoulder. Inside the building was not pitch dark, the doors had frosted glass windows at the top, just a narrow strip posing no security risk and on the back wall was a strip of glass bricks. Even so he would need the torch he had brought to see well enough to check the place out; he'd decided that he wouldn't risk putting the light on though he had seen a switch on the wall just inside the door. He took in his surroundings for a moment, he had entered near the back of a white van, driven in nose first and which he saw had the words Holmes & Son: Locksmiths and a telephone number inscribed on its rear doors and sides. Maybe there was something in there, though he thought that hiding anything in the van might be way too obvious. Given the criminal activities Short now assumed Marty carried out he reckoned that it must have crossed his mind that one day his lock up might well be searched.

Nevertheless, he walked around the van, tried the door and found it locked. No surprise there. He did a circuit round the whole space, noting the other car, which he presumed to be the classic one he knew Marty had driven to Godwin's house on the night of his break in, and finding that locked too. Again no surprise. Along the back wall there were some open metal shelves strewn with a variety of things, large and small, and all to do with cars. There were paint pots, paint brushes, engine oil, polish, jam jars holding nuts and bolts and the like in a huge range of sizes and a huge number of tools. It all seemed to Short to be a bit of an excessive set up just to do a bit of maintenance on an old car and a small basic Ford van, but then the constable was not thinking of Marty's passion for work as a renovator. He rummaged a bit along the back wall but there seemed no possibility of finding anything interesting among the shelves.

Also set against the back wall was a jumbo-sized metal trunk, it was old and rusted but the padlock on it wasn't old, it was clean and suggested that the trunk was in regular use. Short opened it up, using the bolt cutters again, tossed the lock aside and opened the lid. Despite having high hopes that this might be what he was after, he was disappointed. The trunk proved to be just a glorified cupboard for things that might be used while someone was working on the vehicles: there was an electric kettle, its use made possible by a water tap and sink that he had noticed fixed on one wall, some mugs, all of which had seen better days, their inside surfaces stained dark brown with caffeine, hand cleaning gel the label on which boasted it would remove oil in a flash and even a tin of biscuits. Short checked the biscuit tin to find it contained nothing but the biscuits indicated on the lid.

If there was anything at all secreted here, and he had not given up on that possibility yet, it seemed that one of the vehicles remained as the last possible hiding place. He knew a bit about how cars were stolen and felt that getting into them would present him with no real problem. He was about to break into the van when he stopped and stood stock still; if light bulbs did go off magically over peoples' heads one would have hovered above him at that moment. He had given up on Marty's ambiguous note, now discarded, but he now thought he knew what it had meant – *look under my favourite thing.* It was the car, surely it was the old car. He ignored the van and walked round it to the Jowett. He didn't know of the name and had never seen one before. He shone his torch up and down and it was clear that the car was in immaculate condition. The paint gleamed, the chrome shone. He wondered what something like that might be worth, conjuring up a figure of several, perhaps many, thousands of pounds which, was he but to know, was very close to the true value. For a moment he considered stealing the car if all else failed, he was desperate, but a very little thought persuaded him that that was a poor idea as the vehicle was too rare, and thus would be easy to track, recognise and trace.

He crouched down alongside the car. Underneath. Now he might be getting somewhere. An old tarpaulin was spread under the car, frayed and replete with the oil of use over many years, on it was a battered blue metal toolbox, which when he opened it proved to contain nothing but the tools for which it was designed. There was also quite a lot of junk: enough crisp packets to start a collection, a single old number plate and a set of red trade plates, plus an assortment of loose nuts and bolts and the like, all of which led him to presume the tarpaulin was there to catch such small detritus when the car was being worked on.

There was also a kind of long metal tray on wheels, Short did not know what such devices were called, but he knew they allowed someone to lie on them and pull themselves under a vehicle to get at and work on anything there that needed attention. Feeling he was onto something, and ignoring the fact that he was going to get pretty dirty in the process, he used it to inspect the underneath of the Jowett. It took him a while as he had to move the creeper device several times to make sure he examined the whole under-surface of the car. He shone his torch to and fro. Even with the little he knew about cars, he could see that this car had been subject to loving renovation, he could not imagine any car being cleaner underneath, but he found no secret hiding place and nothing small either like a key in a magnetic box.

He pulled himself out and stood up, then as he did so he realised that the floor below the car was not concrete; something gave a little and moved under his foot. Pulling the creeper out of the way he tugged the tarpaulin aside and pushed it into a crumpled heap against the back wall of the lock up. That done he found he had exposed what appeared to be a long row of boards. He banged one, got a hollow sound, and realised they were covering an inspection pit. *Underneath my favourite thing.* Now he was more convinced that he was onto something, desperate to get his hands on some money and with the deadline for payment fast approaching he knew that letting down the sort of people to whom he owed the money was very much not to be recommended. He knew that next time spilt coffee would be the least of his problems; it was a thought that was clouding his judgement.

It took a while to get the first board out; he missed the fact that one board had a hole drilled through it to enable it to be lifted up with one finger. He got an old screwdriver from the shelves along the back wall and prized one board up, once the first one was out he could get a grip on the next and he very soon had perhaps two thirds of them removed and stacked in front of the car. A length of old wooden ladder to facilitate entrance was visible, he shone his torch down, the pit was quite deep and contained a good many things. As well as a fair amount of litter – more crisp packets – there were a number of bits from cars: an old wheel without its tyre, a battered old car seat, and various small car parts Short could not identify. At the narrow ends of the pit what appeared to be plywood boards stood upright wedged into each end on which were displayed a variety of tools hung from hooks.

He was about to clamber down the ladder and have a proper look in the pit when he was surprised as the door of the lockup was swung open wide, bright daylight streamed in to illuminate him and someone shouted at him.

"What the bloody hell are you doing here?" He looked across and saw the figure of Tracy Hines standing in the doorway staring at him; even from a few yards away he could see the flash of anger in her eyes.

Chapter Twenty-Four
Sounds like a plan.

Earlier that day Tracy had been having a busy morning, including spending far too long trying to persuade an elderly man that buying a new padlock was a much better course of action than her trying to locate a replacement key for something that looked like it had been used to lock up prehistoric caves. Despite her best efforts he had decided to "have one more look around for the key" before deciding and he had departed empty handed.

Work had been pretty full on for a while now as Tracy coped with the shop on her own. But she felt she was managing. Things had started well with the arrangement with Steve, she had already taken on two or three jobs that she had no idea how to do, they had attended together and she had watched as he worked. He was not quite as clear as Marty had been in his explanations and instruction, but she had found the arrangement did work, and she was sure that it would help her expand what she could do by working with him. Time would tell, she thought, but it was very much a question of so far so good. The progress made prompted another thought, that maybe one day she would need an assistant. There was a limit to how much time she could allow the shop to be closed while she did outside work; she resolved to give the matter some thought.

She did not want to rush things with Mary, who after all was grieving and doubtless had so many things to cope with alongside that uncertain process, but they had sorted out most things regarding the shop for the moment and Tracy kept telling her everything was fine and they could leave deciding any final details for the moment. Mary on the other hand had repeated several times that she was finding it helped her to keep busy, and Tracy got regular texts from her written as various random thoughts struck her. The most recent said: Added Jim to insurance for van. Do use whenever. Business or pleasure.

A kind thought, the pleasure bit, Tracy decided as she acknowledged the message with a thank you and found as she did so that she had begun to follow Mary's pattern of writing texts: a little bit spare perhaps, but no abbreviations and no faces or symbols. She even put a full stop at the end.

The shop kept her busy all morning and just when she was thinking of taking a break, grabbing a sandwich to bring in so that the shop was not left unattended for too long, her phone pinged to signal the receipt of a text. This one was from Jim: Meet for lunch? See you at 1.

A bit of assumption going on there she thought and not the most fluent of writers, nevertheless she felt a break would do no harm and replied agreeing to his suggestion. They both knew where to meet, Marty's favourite café had become their usual haunt in the market. Half an hour later, she had been greeted as she entered the café as she had been every day since his passing by someone saying: "Getting on alright without Marty?" Such acted as a constant reminder of how he had been regarded by the locals and she knew such remarks were well meant. Once they had met up and found a table in the busy café, she sat opposite Jim, each with a sandwich and a mug in front of them, both feeling pleased to be having a break, albeit a short one, rather than restricting themselves to a quick bite on the job and pausing little from their work.

"You're working too hard, you deserve a break," said Jim, taking a line he had spent time rehearsing.

"I'm fine, why do say that?"

"Well two reasons: first because things have hardly been normal for you of late, ever since Marty died you've been working like a maniac to keep that shop going and working with Steve too to increase the range of things you do. Plus there is all the shop admin to do. It must be a huge load. Go on, admit it."

"Okay, you're right, it has been busy, but I'm not just an employee now, it's worth my while to keep the business going and get it growing. Besides, any success will pay me well. Mary's being very generous about the new arrangements and she just lets me get on with it. After what she's been through I want to do her proud." Tracy paused, bit into her sandwich and chewed for a while, then adding: "But... hang on, what was the second reason?"

"I understand what you're saying and of course it's all very much an opportunity. I do get that. But you have to pace yourself a bit. And the second reason's different. I want to see more of you, is that something you can make room for?" Tracy flashed him a broad smile.

"Oh yes, for sure." Jim was well pleased with her rapid response.

"There you are then, what say you we make a start on that today? If we both knock off a bit early we could go to a film and have a meal out as well. All I ever seem to do is eat a sandwich with you." He gave her a quizzical look, hoping very much that her answer would be a yes. He found his feelings for her strengthening, and she surprised him often as they spent more time together and he got to know her better. He liked her and was keen to nurture the relationship into something significant. Tracy knew he was right, she knew very well that she had been burning the candle at both ends with work, and however good the reasons for that might be she thought a break might be both good and well deserved. Furthermore, although they had said little to each other about their friendship they were in fact of similar mind about it. They both wanted it to grow and that meant taking it seriously.

"Okay Jim, you win, that would be nice… and you're right I guess, and while I have an opportunity, I don't want work to become a chore. Marty took quite a chance on me and I'd like to prove he was right, but there are limits. Tell you what, I've got a callout booked, mid-afternoon. I need to go down towards the city, to a shop near Moorgate, and I planned to do that in the van – after that? I could give you a buzz when I've finished."

"How long a call, d'you reckon?"

"Not long, half an hour maybe – though it might take that long to find a place to park! But I need the van 'cos I'm delivering back a safe. Why?"

"Well, how about this? If I come with you, I can sit in the van and fend off traffic wardens for a while as you work, then we could go to a film at the Barbican, that'll be close. I'll check the films and times. Sounds like a plan to me." Tracy reckoned it did too.

"Okay, yes… right, meet me at the lock-up at, say, four. By the way, you know the plan is to sell Marty's old car, his pet renovation project, that is. Mary reckons it's worth a fair bit in the state he'd got it into. He was an artist at that. You could have a look, you might be able to help with getting it sold, though I'm not yet sure what Mary plans. Then we can go on from there. Oh and book us a film, you choose, but nothing depressing or with sub-titles or zombies, right? I must get back to the shop now if that's what's happening later." They both took a last swallow from their mugs and headed back to their respective work.

Little did they realise that the arrangement they had made would not work out quite as planned. Tracy shut up shop early and in good time, collected up the papers about the safe, now repaired, that she had to return and made sure the trolley was ready to transfer it to the van when she parked it at the end of the road. She then headed for the lock-up. Once there she could see from a few paces away that something was wrong, the door was pulled to as if closed, but the lock, a hefty padlock, was nowhere to be seen, it seemed clear that someone had broken in. Tracy went forward intent on seeing what damage might have been done inside. It did not occur to her that the perpetrator might still be present.

Chapter Twenty-Five

I can't believe it

The shock they felt was mutual and for a few seconds Tracy and the interloper, who she at once recognised as Constable Short, just stared at each other without saying a word. Tracy had not expected to find anyone there, much less the rogue policeman, but she was not going to back down. She spoke up first, in more of a shout.

"What the bloody hell are you doing here?" Short said nothing, he was faced with the fact that he had not given enough consideration to what he was doing, and certainly not to what he should do if he was disturbed. After her initial bravado, Tracy found a realisation of her vulnerability dawned on her fast. The policeman had, she believed, had no authority when he had confronted her at the shop, now, having cut through the padlock, which she could see lying on the floor just inside the door, she felt certain he had no authority to do that here either. And he'd hit her once already. She spotted an iron spike lying alongside the second door, which was still closed; it was something Marty had used to prop the doors back while he drove out. She stooped and grabbed it, holding it out a little in front of her as one might a knife. After a long pause Short spoke up.

"I mean to find his ill-gotten gains... one way or another and it will take more than that to stop me." He pointed a finger indicating the spike she now held. This was his last hope, he saw no other way of getting the money he was in such desperate need of in time. An idea struck him:

"We could search together, we could share what we find, come on - think what that could mean." She did not expect that and could read the desperation in his face.

"You don't know that there is anything to find, here or anywhere else; I don't think there is and I've never heard a safe mentioned."

"There must be one, and if you don't help I'll have to...." His voice tailed off as he saw the figure of a man come into view behind her. He was outnumbered. Tracy heard Jim approaching behind her and turned, saying his name.

"What's going on here then?" He asked her.

"It's our rogue policeman, you know, he's convinced Marty had a stash of goodies hidden somewhere in here. He broke in."

"Come on, that's enough, I'll phone the police - you've got to put a stop this." Jim got his mobile phone out of his jeans, but Tracy raised a hand, letting the spike holding one drop to her side.

"Hang on... I don't think we want the police involved again. It's... it's... I don't know what to think." Tracy's voice faltered and Short saw an opportunity and addressed Jim.

"I suggested a deal, we look together and share the spoils we find, you too, I guess, what do you think? It's possible there's a considerable amount here somewhere." At this point Jim put his phone away and advanced into the lock up, Short still stood between the two vehicles, alongside the Jowett. He walked forward so that he was level with the back of the car.

"Otherwise, I'm sure I can think of some charge that will get you out of the way." His voice was harsh, as he offered a stick alongside the carrot of sharing, and he stepped forward as he spoke. It was a move Jim at once interpreted as a threat, after all the man had already resorted to violence against Tracy once and his desperation was plain to see; he stepped between Short and Tracy to protect her and shouted, his voice sudden and loud.

"Not another step! Back off." Jim was a fit looking young man and it was Short who now felt threatened, he turned and moved back, retreating between the cars with Jim following a few steps behind him and maintaining the distance between them as Tracy moved forward too. The truth was none of the three of them had a clear idea of what to do next. Short was desperate, his one feeling that there must be a way to gain what he wanted from the situation. Tracy was anxious not to get involved with the police again and wondered again what anything like that happening would mean for Mary. Jim was in protective mode, his one intention being to keep Short away from Tracy in case he became violent again.

It happened in an instant.

With Jim still close behind him Short glanced over his shoulder and took another step further away from him as he moved between the two vehicles. With his eyes on Jim he put his left foot down and stepped onto the centre of the creeper, which he had earlier moved out from under the car to let him get at the inspection pit. It was as if he had stepped on a skateboard, maybe not so fast, but even so it moved with sudden speed. He flew over in a manner devoid of any control, his feet were thrown up and his whole body became parallel with the ground. In other circumstances he would have landed on his backside in a manner reminiscent of someone slipping on a banana skin. However the positioning here was askew, the creeper was at an angle pointing under the van and shot off in that direction, so that when Short was thrown backwards he did not land on his backside, rather the sudden movement landed him on thin air. He yelled out in shock as he fell six feet into the inspection pit. The whole motion took perhaps two seconds.

The sound of his landing made a fair old thump, and what proved a short yell of surprise was cut off in an instant. There was almost a double thump: it ended with a sound like an axe splitting a log. Both Tracy and Jim drew in an audible breath and Tracy followed that with a louder gasp. In the silence that followed they stepped forward and peered over the lip of the pit. Down below Short lay on his back unmoving. His head had hit the sharp metal rim of a tyre-less car wheel that was lying flat on the floor of the pit and already a fair amount of blood was evident. It was Jim that spoke first.

"Do you think he's dead?"

"I don't know, there's no sign of life, but we have to check. He's a right bastard but we have to do something." She stepped towards the corner of the pit where the ladder rested and made to descend.

"No, no... not you. I'll go." He slipped past her and they both remained silent as he climbed down and stood alongside the prone still figure. Tracy felt strong approval for the way Jim had taken the lead. Jim crouched down and felt Short's wrist and also put his fingers across his neck.

"No pulse that I can feel, but I've never done this before. Do you have a mirror?" Tracy checked her bag, which had hung round her neck ever since she had first approached the lock up door. She confirmed that she had and Jim asked her to pass it down to him. She crouched down, lent over, he reached up and took it from her and then he held it under Short's nose for what seemed to Tracy like forever. He said nothing, passed the mirror back to her and climbed with care back up the ladder.

"Now we have to report it – I'm as sure as I can be - he's dead." He saw the expression on Tracy's face and added: "Come here you." They stood in a silent embrace for a moment, then Jim broke apart.

"Right, this is what we'll do, we'll allow ourselves one white lie to make it easier, to help keep you out of it. We were meeting here. That's true. I got here first, saw the broken lock and came in to check things out, I exchanged a few words with

Short to try and find out what he was doing, he turned and retreated between the van and the car and bingo the creeper sent him into the pit. That's all almost true and the last thing's spot on. Then you arrived, so you can have had no possible involvement. We should keep you right out of it. You better start by saying you know him from the hospital and there may be no need for any more explanation."

"Okay, I guess that does no harm, it's very close to the truth and makes further inquiries about Marty that much less likely, I have to think of Mary too, right?" Jim nodded, he punched 999 into his phone and was asked which service he wanted. He asked for an ambulance first, saying there had been an accident, a fall, he thought someone was dead but couldn't be sure. And police too he specified as he mentioned a break in. He described where they were. The response did not take long.

The ambulance arrived first, and he showed the crew where Short had fallen. One of the team climbed down and verified that he was dead and by the time that was done there was a police car outside too. Asked what had happened Jim's response was encompassed in a few sentences.

"He was here when I arrived, he'd broken in - then the whole thing was over in a few moments." Jim described Short's fall, then added: "I wonder if he was after the car, it's a classic. Must be worth a bob or two." Tracy explained her presence at what for her was part of her workplace. She kept muttering "I can't believe it" and in due course was allowed to return to the shop to get another padlock so that the lock up could be made secure again. Following Jim's lead she explained the need for this by referring to the classic car. Whilst at the shop she phoned her customer to put off the scheduled safe delivery until the following day. All the necessary procedures, along with an examination of the site and the arrival of a hearse shaped van from the morgue, took some time. Tracy arrived back with the new lock as the body, now zipped into a bag, was being carried out of the lockup. At last it was all done.

Once they were again alone Jim gave Tracy another hug.

"I have to say knowing you never has a dull moment. Do you think Marty did have a secret hiding place?"

"I don't know, I don't think so, but if he did then I don't know where it is. Marty wouldn't have told me, now would he? Look around you, there's nothing here." She cast her eyes around the interior of the lock up. And she added: "Look over there. Short even broke into that metal trunk thing and do you know what's kept in there?" Jim shook his head.

"The most valuable thing in that to my certain knowledge is an old kettle. Marty locked up everything. There's often some biscuits in there too, we might rescue those or they'll go stale." She went over, retrieved the tin and then checked her watch.

"Come on, let's lock up here, it's late now. Too late to deliver that safe, I rang them from the shop. I guess the cinema will have to wait for another evening too, I wonder if you can change the tickets? Well done for mentioning the car, good idea that, gives him a motive and half the market knows about Marty's fixation with old cars. But so much for your attempt to get me to ease up a bit." She grinned and Jim responded in kind.

"Expect me to go on working on that, come on let's get back." They walked together towards the market and Jim persuaded Tracy to have a quick bite and a nightcap at a pub on Islington Green. He had an ulterior motive for their having a chat and after they had further reviewed the events of the day, he came out with it.

"Tracy, I wonder, well, what I mean to say is…" He paused and Tracy commented.

"You're not this tongue tied as a rule, what is it, a confession of some sort? What have you been up to?"

"Up to? No, no, all good I hope. Okay I'll just say it. How would you feel about us getting a flat together, I reckon we get on well, really well, I hate it when you go back to your Mum's place rather than mine, what do you think?" Tracy did not receive his question with much surprise, and indeed she was pleased, but she still felt she needed a moment.

"It's a bit late for a bombshell like that and I promised Mum I wouldn't be too late tonight. Can we talk about it later?"

"Hmm, is that getting me ready for a no?"

"No, no it's not, just, well, it's late and…well, we've just witnessed a death." Her voice tailed off.

"Of course, okay, you would have to be sure, and I know you have a lot going on right now, but at least now you'll have no more trouble from your rogue cop to distract you - give my suggestion your full attention please." They parted with Tracy promising to do just that, both unaware of the further distractions that lay ahead.

Chapter Twenty-Six

Very much in the past

Many miles away from London, Beth sprayed sun tan oil onto her legs and rubbed it in. For some reason it was a process she hated. Of course almost all the oil disappeared after a while and she realised it was a strange thing to dislike. After all, her nursing job had her dealing with much worse on a daily basis: blood, puss and vomit were the least of it, plus miscellaneous spillages of food and drink. Despite all this, she loved her job and for the most part characterised it as helping people, helping people who were in difficulty, she liked that, she reckoned she made a difference. She rubbed her hands to and fro on a damp corner of her towel to get rid of the last of the oil.

She sat up on the sunbed, the water of a swimming pool sparkling in front of her, and a cocktail of some sort stood on the table alongside her, one that the barman had insisted was: "...very mild, mainly coconut". It wasn't. Beyond the pool there was an uninterrupted view across the ocean. The sun shone down on Lanzarote and she was very grateful for the break, a last minute cut-price deal taken with Shelly and her boyfriend with whom she shared a small apartment not too far from the hospital. All three friends worked at the hospital, albeit in different roles: a nurse, a lab technician and a receptionist.

It was only when she got away like this, or sometimes if her shifts produced a long weekend off, that she realised how stressful her job could often be. Day by day you just kept going, you had to, but any set back, deaths most of all, was upsetting to say the least for the staff, such things went with the territory so to speak and she, like most of her colleagues, had learnt to cope with it. However it was not always easy and some things like the death of a child left more of a mark. The good things outweighed the bad though in her opinion. She took a sip from her strange drink, wondering how anything that was such a bright pink could be 'mostly coconut'. She got up, tossed her towel back on the lounger and moved towards the pool.

"Anyone else coming for a dip?" She called out as she stepped forward and then, hearing no reply, she dived into the water. Behind her neither of her friends moved. As she swam she reflected that there had been a death on the ward on her last day at work before the holiday: Marty Holmes, a patient who stuck in her memory because he had been in some sort of trouble with the police.

As ever it was very sad, but this week there would be nothing like that, just sun, sea and who knew what. She did rather believe she had invested a more than adequate sum in her bikini to guarantee a good holiday. As she struck out along the pool, the promise she had made to Marty to pass on his message had slipped her memory.

In the aftermath of the drama at the lock up Tracy worried that Constable Short's visit to Marty's premises might result in someone thinking that there was more to be investigated. But in fact the matter seemed to reach a swift conclusion. In London the local police were convinced of his death being an accident and normal procedures locked in and were followed. In the process of dealing with the body his identification and the fact that he had been a policeman was soon discovered. His death was reported to both his parents with whom he still lived and the powers that be at the police station in which he worked. Apart from the fact that he was a policeman the incident was seen as being routine.

As soon as the circumstances were known at his station out in Essex various questions were asked, most about what he had been doing in a garage in Islington. The possible theft of a classic car seemed an odd possibility until, as was inevitable in such a situation, the formal side of the questioning met the prevailing station gossip head on. Constable Short was well known amongst his colleagues to have had a gambling problem and it did not take long to discover that he was in trouble over what was a considerable debt. A debt it soon became clear that was becoming due very soon to a well-known and disreputable lender. Given who it was discovered that he had run up the debt with, it was clear that he had been a desperate man, one who might very well have resorted to theft. Despite his occupation an intended theft seemed at once plausible. The story of an officer meeting his death while undertaking a crime was not something his superiors wanted to see get wide publicity. So before very long his death became a private matter for his family, and only a small number from the station attended his funeral. A brief item in the local newspaper reported that he had met is death in a fall and had not been on duty at the time.

If anyone made a link with Marty Holmes, no one dwelt on it at any length and the fact that the death had occurred in an area under the jurisdiction of one police authority and that Short had worked in another clouded the issue and would have made further liaison between the forces time consuming. Besides it was classified as just being an unfortunate accident and an incident that needed no further investigation. The formalities were soon past and the matter was then regarded as being best forgotten; it was soon regarded as being very much in the past.

One good thing did result: a while after the accident the attention of the police in Loughton focused for a moment on a certain well known unauthorised money lender and that did lead to a renewed investigation of their practices and evidence of the violent tactics that were part of their regular money retrieval tactics. In due course it led to several arrests and, later, to convictions.

Chapter Twenty-Seven

It's a car

After an enjoyable and refreshing holiday, on returning to the hospital Beth felt awful. She prided herself on being well organised, and on being caring too, after all that was her profession. Yet when she returned from her holiday, went back to the hospital to start her first shift and opened up her locker, the first thing she saw was a scrappy note stuck to the inside of the door with Sellotape. She had written:

Marty Holmes. Tell Tracy to look under his favourite thing.

Then on a new line by way of reminder:

Works at locksmiths in Chapel Market. Says she'll figure it out. Tell her that too.

She kicked herself, she had forgotten all about her promise in the rush to get ready to go away on holiday and a whole week had gone by. Her shift dictated an early start, so she resolved to go to the shop later to apologise and pass the message on without further delay and thought the timing would allow her to get the tube and reach the locksmith's shop to be there before it closed.

Tracy was just about to shut up shop for the day and leave, she had already raised the hatch to let herself out from behind the counter when the shop bell rang, and a young woman came in. Tracy stayed behind the counter but spoke up first:

"I was just closing up, whatever you want I'm sorry, but it might have to wait until tomorrow. How can I help?" The woman smiled at her.

"I am in the right place, you're Tracy right, I recognise you."

"Yes, hang on… you're the nurse that looked after Marty aren't you, I'm sorry I don't remember your name."

"I am, it's Beth, and I'm afraid I owe you a huge apology. Marty asked me to give you a message – 'in case anything happened to him' he said. A number of people in hospital say that and in most cases they're fine but in his case something did happen to him of course, so sad, he seemed like a nice man, and he wasn't so old. Anyway I've been on holiday, on the day he asked me I was getting ready to go away the following morning. I've been away for a week – Lanzarote it was. Sorry, I'm prattling on. The thing is I've got a message for you. I saw my reminder note as soon as I opened my locker this morning. It was stuck to the door. If I had not gone away I would never have forgotten."

"Right, thanks, the delay probably doesn't matter given how things worked out. What was the message?" Beth opened her handbag and rummaged about inside a little before producing a crumpled piece of paper.

"Let me get this exactly right, 'cos I don't know what it means, he just said 'Tell Tracy to look under my favourite thing'." She put the note down on the counter. "Oh, and he said to tell you that you would figure it out."

"Well, I'm not sure it means anything to me either, I better give it some thought, he must have felt it was important I guess. Anyway, thanks, it was kind of you to come round with it, I hope you haven't gone too much out of your way. The least I can do is offer you a drink, do you fancy a visit to the pub? I've finished here for the day." Beth hesitated, but then agreed, saying that she wished more of her patients asked her to run errands if a drink was what followed when they were done. Ensconced with glasses in front of them in the nearest pub, which was just beginning to get busy at the end of the day, Tracy proposed a vote of thanks.

"Cheers and thank you for bringing the message and for everything you did for Marty in hospital, it's just a pity he didn't make it." She realised at once that did not sound quite right and added: "Not that what happened was in any way your fault, of course."

"Yes, well, that's strokes for you. He seemed like a nice man." The comment made Tracy smile as she recollected her old boss. If he had sent her a message it must, she thought, have some importance. It was a puzzle.

"He was, he helped me so much, gave me a job – me with hardly a qualification to my name and a dire record of mucking up dead end jobs – and he helped me learn a trade, it's quite a technical business too. Let me know if you ever want to get into a safe." They both laughed.

"Tell me something about him. What was all that police business?"

"Well he was a nice man as I say, saw me alright, he'd been married for ever, I think you met his wife, Mary, when she visited the hospital. She's very cut up, but she's been a star about the shop, letting me go on running it and seeing to all the financial arrangements. And there is no way Marty murdered anyone. End of. Now he's gone I doubt we'll ever know the full story, but I'm sure, he was a good man, he was the only one there when someone died, he was just in the wrong place at the wrong time and, as I say, he helped me so much. But his real passion was cars."

"Cars? In what way?"

"He bought old wrecks; his wife always called them 'his old bangers' but he called them 'classics'. He renovated them and sold them on, it was doing the work on them he loved and he was a real perfectionist, he… wait a minute, I bet that's what the message means. His favourite thing… I know what that message means. It's the car! Look under the car. Gosh I'm doubly grateful to you now, without this conversation I might have puzzled over what that meant for ages. I hope I'm right."

They chatted on for a while until Beth said she had to get on, they exchanged numbers and promised to keep in touch.

Once Beth had gone Tracy got her phone out and sent Jim a short text message:
New development. Meet me at lock up.

Jim replied to say he was on his way and half an hour later they met up outside the lock up, where Jim found Tracy already unlocking the door.

"What's all this about? Where's the fire?" Jim had responded without delay to Tracy's message and they had arrived moments apart in the alley. He wanted to know what the panic was. Tracy explained about having a visit from Beth, about her delivering a message from Marty and why there had been a delay before she had done so. She opened the lock up door.

"Never mind, good of her to remember at all I guess. What was this message then?" Jim asked.

"It meant nothing to me at first but as we chatted and as I talked about Marty it came to me: *look under my favourite thing* he said. His favourite thing – it's the old car, it's got to be. Do you think he had something hidden away after all? It had to be something he did not want ignored if anything happened to him or he wouldn't have bothered sending a message like that." Jim led the way into the lock up, switching on the light as he went in. Tracy pulled the door to behind her.

"Well, who knows, but we may be going to find out. For the moment I have only one thing to say: be careful and don't go falling into that pit. There's been enough drama in here to last us both a lifetime." Tracy overtook him and walked between the two vehicles.

"Let's take a look, can you grab that light?" She pointed to a hand held lamp, the bulb set under a sort of metal cage for protection and attached to a long length of wire plugged into a socket on the back wall. Jim got hold of it, switched it on and clambered down the ladder first with the lamp sending light flashing to and fro as he did so. He turned at the bottom and helped Tracy as she followed him down the ladder. For a moment they just stood looking at each other, Tracy noticed that there was still some of Constable Short's dried blood on the floor and the old wheel. She pointed at it.

"We should do something about that, right?"

Jim agreed then played the lamp over the underside of the car directing it foot by foot from end to end.

"It's like it was new," said Jim craning his neck, "but I can't see anything else, can you?" Tracy had to admit that she couldn't. Jim even shone the lamp into the exhaust pipe; he found nothing.

"It's very odd," she said, "Marty was so precise about things, it seems he wanted to disguise what he was saying, after all the police were there with him all the time he was in the hospital, remember, but he must have meant something, and he must have thought I would know what he meant. I wonder if we are actually on the right track. Did he have something else he thought of as more favourite than this?" They stood in silence for a while and Jim swung the lamp to and fro again beneath the car; still nothing jumped out at them. Then, as he swung the light right around the pit he had an idea.

"The message said 'under the car' but not on it. Maybe there's something else down here we're missing." He stamped hard on the floor, but the concrete seemed as hard and solid as one would expect.

"I can't think what, unless his stash was something that would go in an old crisp packet, he was an untidy old bugger wasn't he?" Jim shone the light around again.

"Wait a minute. This pit is concrete lined isn't it, do you think the boards at the ends where the tools are hung move? They might well have been put in later. Let's see." He took a large screwdriver off a hook on the board at one end of the pit and, without waiting for Tracy to comment, he started to prise the board away from the wall. Tracy couldn't help feel it was not the right use for such a tool but, eager for an answer, she said nothing. She knew that Marty would have stopped such inappropriate and damaging use in a moment; he was a stickler for the care of his precious tools. Jim struggled for a bit until the board came loose from where it was jammed in tight, it tilted and some of the tools hanging on it spilled onto the floor. He pulled the thing aside. All it revealed was a dusty concrete wall.

"Nothing," said Tracy once they were sure nothing useful had been discovered. "Try the other end?" Jim pushed the board back into place and, to wedge it tight, he whacked in one of the top corners with the handle end of the screwdriver making Tracy wince. She had picked up some of Marty's habits over the time she had worked with him, indeed he had been at pains to see that she did so. Jim then moved past her and went through the same motions at the other end of the pit. This time the board was easier to move and, once one corner was loose, they saw that it was fastened to hidden hinges on the other side.

"This looks more like it," said Tracy as Jim got his fingers under it and the wooden panel swung open almost like a door. Well," she went on, "I was wondering why he sent the message to me and not to Mary, now I guess I know the reason. Look. She'd never have got into that!"

In front of them, set flush into the concrete wall, was the unmistakable door of a safe.

Chapter Twenty-Eight

Marty would have been pleased

With already half the evening gone Tracy declared it too late to do more, not least on a rumbling empty stomach, so they had closed up the wall in the pit, rehung the tools that had fallen to the floor and resolved to explore further the following day. She locked the door and they walked out of the alley.

"It would have been no good getting a message to Mary about this, she couldn't get in there even if she found the safe. Marty knew – or hoped - I could open it and he trusted me too, I guess. Anyway, I hope I can in fact open it, this is not a job I want to share with Steve." Tracy was recapping their discovery.

"Will you tell Mary about this?" Jim asked as they walked back towards the market. Tracy thought about it for a second or two and made a rapid decision.

"Yes… yes, I must. We don't know what's inside the safe yet, it may be nothing, or it may contain instructions about whatever it is, either way I'll tell her. But let's see if I can open it first and find out what's inside."

"Whatever it is I bet Mary will be surprised," Jim offered, though he knew much less of Mary than did Tracy.

"Oh no, no surprise, she and Marty were married for more than thirty years and I know she knew about what she called his little expeditions even before they got married. Let's forget tomorrow and leave this till Sunday, I need time - I may well not be able to get into that safe in just my lunch break." Jim agreed and before going to their separate homes they agreed to meet and talk about it all at lunchtime the following day. Before going to bed Tracy sent Mary a quick text message:
I need to talk to you, are you free on Sunday?

The following day they found there was not much more to say, until the safe was open every possibility was mere speculation. Any further decisions would have to wait.

On Saturday, unable to contain their impatience and curiosity for any longer, Tracy closed the shop ahead of time and they set off to the lock up. Jim carried a heavy bag over his shoulder containing tools Tracy had selected for the job of opening the safe, she carried a bag with a flask in it and a couple of mugs too; she had said the job might take a while and she described the mugs that lived at the lock up as being old, disgusting and a light year away from any sort of cleanliness. She opened up the lock up and they went inside, pulling the door closed behind them.

"Okay, thanks for coming with me, Jim, but you'll need to let me get on with it for a while, it's not a two hander job. I'm still not sure whether I can do this, the safe's by no means new, it's probably been here for years, it might even be that his father put it in, but it's for sure not something I'm familiar with, and it's a good safe, Marty wouldn't have put up with anything else though would he?"

"I guess not, don't worry but let me go down into the pit first, I would prefer to be at the bottom to guide you down. No more accidents, eh." Tracy agreed, Jim descended the ladder and she passed the bag to him before climbing down herself. They opened up the end wall again, pulling back the thick plywood sheet as before and then, on Tracy's prompting, Jim climbed back up to floor level, he found an old stool in the corner and pulled it into a position where he could speak to Tracy without shouting. She shouted up to him almost before he had got settled.

"Can you put the plug on, you know so this lamp works." That done she cut off any attempt he made at conversation with a loud shush and he sat in silence finding things to do on his phone. An hour went by with few words spoken, although he could see the light change and flashes shoot up out of the pit as she changed her position and moved the lamp; at one point she dropped something metal on the concrete floor with a clang. Then another hour passed during which the regularity and volume of Tracy's curses now broke the silence and escalated in frequency as time went by. Finally daring to interrupt Jim persuaded her to take a break.

"You'll go boss eyed down there, come up and have a drink." She surfaced and as Jim poured them both a coffee he could see Tracy was not too happy, a fact confirmed as she banged down her mug sending splashes of coffee shooting onto the floor.

"It's an absolute pig. By that I mean it's a very good safe. As I said, I would expect no less of Marty but… it's frustrating and annoying and… it's just not working. I've been trying to manipulate it, but the wheel pack – that's the central mechanism of a combination lock – has taken a dislike to me. I hoped I could use just a stethoscope, but that's an overrated trick, it's really only guaranteed to work in the movies. I could drill it, if I can reach the drive cam I could…" Her voice tailed off and Jim found he had little idea what to say and besides he didn't understand the technical terms she had used. After a few minutes silence she went on, now sounding a little more bullish.

"I have spent half the time just staring at the thing thinking of how not to proceed. The trouble is I need to know more about this safe, as I've said it's not a model I have ever come across before and it's a good one. There is no point in drilling blind, I don't know where to aim. Let's leave it for now, if I spend some time on the internet to check and find details about it then it may go better when I start again in the morning."

They closed up in the pit again rendering the safe invisible and climbed up and went on their way. When Jim suggested going to his place he was pleased to find that Tracy agreed without hesitation. They ordered and ate a takeaway – a pizza – then Tracy started researching on Jim's computer, a process that involved a regular shush as far as Jim was concerned if he tried to interject. It was late before he could tear her away from her research, but she said it had all been time well spent. She had made copious notes and printed out a couple of diagrams and expressed some confidence that she would get it right on the next attempt.

The following morning, they returned to the lock up. Jim had switched on the power for the lamp and again went down the ladder first to assist Tracy climb down without mishap and help open up the end wall again so as to give access to the safe. Once all was set, Tracy took a deep breath.

"Okay, let's have another go." She said "I'll give it my best shot." Jim stood motionless facing away from her; he appeared not to have heard her speak. "Jim, come on, time to leave me to it for a bit, okay?" He remained facing away from her and ignored her while a few more moments passed before he spoke.

"Have you looked at this board?" He asked as he looked at the inside of the board they had opened up like a door. "It's got pretty grubby over the years, all dust and smears of oil, but there are things written on it. Some of it is illegible, but look. There's a reminder to buy milk, it has a big tick across it so I guess he remembered; I wonder when that was. There's other things too. I quite like this: *Locksmiths are key workers...* and this: *Knowing how to pick locks has opened a lot of doors for me.* Intriguing."

"Yeah, okay, enough for a small smile, I suppose, but I bet it's not as interesting as what may be inside this safe, come on, I should get going."

"Not yet. Just a sec, hang on. You see I've noticed something else, quite low down, I didn't see it at first. Tell me about combinations, if you knew the combination you need how many numbers would it be?"

"But we don't know the number, that's the whole point Dumbo."

"But if you did... what would they..." Tracy was becoming exasperated and interrupted as he paused.

"I don't know. Well, I might I suppose. Yes. I think what is needed would be six two digit numbers, but why... just let me get on eh, I think I learnt where to position the drill last night." Jim turned and beamed at her.

"Six numbers. You know I think Marty may have left us the combination, well not for us in person perhaps, this was done long before he knew you. I think he wrote it down, many years ago by the looks of it, maybe as a reminder for himself or a backup in case something happened to him – who knows? Have a look here." Tracy joined him as he pointed low down on the board. Just visible amongst the mess, dirt and half obscured scribbles was a circle in which was scrawled:

282
930

_____

_____

Two lines stretched across a little below the lower number.

"There, how about that?"

"What are you going on about? That's two three digit numbers and not... well, it's no help at all. Come on."

"Wait. Look at it as a series. The lines here seem to indicate that there's additional numbers to follow on. Okay, what do you reckon logic dictates must come next, what are the next two numbers?" Tracy raised an eyebrow and tutted.

"I have no idea what they are or how this is helping us in any way." Her tone was now impatient and a touch critical and Jim sensed that it would not be right to keep her dangling any longer.

"It's an old trick, add two more numbers: 313 and 233. Now do you see now?"

"Frankly. No. I don't." Jim allowed himself a grin.

"You'll kick yourself when you see what..." Tracy punched him on his arm.

"You... oh, for heaven's sake, just bloody tell me!"

"Okay, see what happens if you read the numbers in sequence... but two at a time. It's two digit numbers we want, right? It says: 28, 29, 30, and when you go further and add on 313 and 233 it's: 28, 29, 30... 31, 32, 33. That's six two digit numbers. Now there's no way that can be a coincidence. It's much too neat. Do you think it looks like Marty's writing?"

"It's messy enough, I suppose, but, but wait… how did you even do that?"

"I've seen it before, this sort of thing, at school, I think. It's quirky and clever and once you've seen it you tend to remember it. Also, I've just thought, remember Marty's message, well the last bit was about figuring it out… numbers… *figures*. See, it does seem to make sense. Surely it's worth a try?" Having taken all this in, Tracy now hesitated not at all, she turned and positioned herself right in front of the safe. With a steady hand, something she found somewhat difficult to achieve in the circumstances, she spun the combination dial to and fro as Jim read out the numbers to her one at a time. The process seemed to take forever but in reality it took no more than a few seconds. When she was rewarded with a satisfying click and the door released Tracy let go of a huge breath she had not realised she was holding. She looked across at Jim and they held each other's gaze for a moment then she pulled the door back revealing the interior of the safe and they found themselves looking at shelves stacked with piles of bank notes banded into neat bundles.

"Look, look. Oh my God, this is more cash than I have ever seen in my whole life!" She said as she turned and flung her arms round Jim crushing him in a tight hug. "You did it, you bloody well did it!"

"No, Marty did it. It was a clever message, he reckoned it would work and it did." Said Jim.

After another hug and a few moments of babbling with excitement at each other simultaneously they calmed down and took stock. Tracy tried to put herself in Marty's shoes.

"I guess he must have always known that there was some possibility that one day he would be caught or that something would curtail his activities. This must have been done a long while back given the state of that wooden board. What a clever old rogue he was."

"Well, having done that he put his trust in you Tracy; Marty would have been pleased that you got in there."

"Yeah, I suppose. He would take some credit for it too, after all I learnt everything from him. Hang on: even though I think I could now break into it, I didn't need to. So credit where credit is due, I'm not sure I would ever have spotted those numbers much less worked out what they showed. Well done you. Let's see what we've found." They did a rough count of the bank notes, some of which were Euros, something that made sense given George Godwin's impending move to Europe, and they also found a velvet bag with a drawer string at the top. When Tracy weighed in in her hand it contained a substantial weight, she peeped inside she could see it contained jewellery, quite a lot of jewellery. All of a sudden Tracy remembered the time; she glanced at her watch and turned to Jim.

"Come on, we'll be late, we're supposed to be at Mary's place soon, I'll take the bag, but we'll lock the safe again for the moment. This promises to be an interesting lunch." They again closed up, moving the board back to hide the safe, and hanging some of the tools back in place on the hooks. Tracy fastened the door with the new padlock she had brought to replace the one the rogue policeman had destroyed to make the place secure.

"You know what?" She said as they set off through the Islington streets. "I reckon Marty would be pretty pleased with our work on this. Good teamwork, eh." They both knew Mary's cooking and reckoned they were in for a treat, though what they had to tell her should be a treat too.

Chapter Twenty-Nine

Now it's down to us

Tracy's message to Mary had triggered a reply inviting both her and Jim to join her for another Sunday lunch. After the surprise of their successful exploration in the pit they made it just in time, arriving at her house as instructed on the dot of twelve o'clock to be greeted by a smiling Mary and the distinctive smell of roasting meat.

"It's nice to see you both, come on in, I'll be ready before too long. I haven't done a proper Sunday roast since Marty was… well, you know… so this is actually a treat for me too. It's lamb, I hope that's okay." They both nodded with enthusiasm and Tracy whispered to Jim: "She's looking a bit better now," as they walked through to the kitchen.

"This is so very good of you," Tracy told Mary, "it must be difficult, well, you know... anyway thanks so much. We've got news for you, we've found that Marty had a safe hidden in the lock up, we need to have a serious talk." Mary waved any such thoughts away, saying that food must come first or it would spoil, she passed Jim back the bottle of red wine he and Tracy had brought together with a corkscrew she got out of one of the kitchen drawers.

"Can you open that up for us, Jim?"

"I'm more used to a bottle opener but, yes, no problem, I'm sure I can get us into it." A few moment's struggle was followed by a satisfying pop and he poured them all a glass of wine. For a few minutes they sat round the table in the dining half of the kitchen chattering about this and that, while Tracy and Jim wondered how Mary could hold off the news until after lunch. Soon an alarm on the cooker sounded. Mary announced it to be a signal that everything was ready, she refused all help at getting things organised, though she did ask if anyone could carve. Jim blanched at the thought, but Tracy volunteered saying that, being brought up by her mother alone, she had been taught to do it at a young age, though her total kitchen skills were not huge.

"Makes sense," said Mary. "Marty always told me you were a dextrous one." She handed over a lethal looking carving knife and fork and Tracy went to work with a vengeance, her skill made evident by how little time she needed to do the job. As they sat down again once everything was ready Mary laid down some house rules.

"Right, remember, no talk of business until lunch is finished please... and I know I've said this in the past, but no phones at the table either, that's always been a rule in this house." It was a splendid lunch even if Tracy and Jim struggled to be patient and keep their minds off their dramatic recent find as Mary regaled them with news of her sister Betty.

"It was good of her to stay until after the funeral, you know. She was a great help with all the arrangements and frankly it was just good not to be alone in the house. She's got more time now since her kids have been at university, though I wonder just what they get up to there now they are independent. I suspect Betty would have a fit. Now, you two all finished?"

Plates were cleared away and more laid out as apple pie appeared to follow the roast; it all had Tracy feeling somewhat ashamed of her own culinary skills by comparison and declaring Mary to be a world class traditional cook, a compliment Mary brushed away by saying it was all 'routine'. Food finished Mary asked if they had eaten enough and turned to the reason for the gathering.

"To business then. Though I have to say that, because I don't know where this will take us, I think perhaps we should only talk about this between the two of us Tracy, no offense, would you mind Jim?" Mary looked from Tracy to Jim as she continued to speak.

"You seem to be, what do you young folk say? An item. If that's so, and I rather hope it is I have to say, it's still quite early days. I've got to know you well Tracy and Marty clearly trusted you with this. It's true to say that I've taken to Jim too, but just for the moment, okay?" Tracy was on the point of arguing but Mary's face seemed to forbid that and she kept quiet; neither of them wanted to upset Mary at such a time. If Jim was disappointed he hid it well and he wondered to himself whether he and Tracy were indeed 'an item' as Mary put it; he hoped so but reckoned there was more to be done in that regard. They still had to talk further about his idea of moving in together. Jim got up from the table.

"Don't worry that's fine, I understand. I'll catch up with you back at mine later Tracy, okay?" As Tracy nodded he hooked his jacket off the back of his chair and headed out into the hall. A moment later they heard the front door click shut.

Mary pushed her chair back and began carrying plates to the sink, Tracy took her share and Mary loaded the dishwasher.

"This was always Marty's job, I'm sure I do it all wrong... but it seems to get everything clean. I'll switch it on when you've gone, it makes a bit of a racket."

They went back to the table and Tracy described their exploits in the pit and what they had discovered that Marty had done to ensure access to the safe in his absence. Mary listened, just nodded every now and then as the story unfolded, and then said "Dear Marty. I did know there was a safe place somewhere, but he kept its location secret even from me, but I might have known he'd have a plan, I'm sure he would not have wanted it to never have been found."

Tracy then explained that she had left the cash locked in the safe, hidden from prying eyes and secure too, but that there was something else that she had brought for Mary to see. She got the black velvet bag of jewellery out of her bag and passed it over. When Tracy had spoken about the cash that was in the safe, Mary had been somewhat dismissive and told her to keep it where it was for the moment, it was the jewellery she wanted to discuss now. Mary undid the drawer strings at the top of the bag and, with due respect for the contents, she tipped the bag and emptied it out spreading the items across the tablecloth. There were more than a dozen separate pieces, some quite elaborate, and all appeared to be gold, with many displaying a healthy amount of diamonds and what appeared to their inexpert eyes to be other precious stones. Mary let out a long, audible breath as she spread the items out further so that each was visible in its own right. They both stared at what was lying on the table and said nothing for several long minutes, then Tracy broke the silence.

"I only glanced into the bag for a moment at the lock up. Now, seeing them spread out in proper light, well they're… they're so beautiful."

"They are indeed. I'm no expert, but their quality seems clear, they're of some considerable age too I'd guess, very special, but they do present us with a problem though."

"Well I know that!" Tracy laughed as she said it. "But a good problem, I think." Mary took off the spectacles she had put on to look at the jewellery and let them hang round her neck on a black cord. She rubbed her eyes and pushed her chair further back from the table.

"Let me explain," she began "As you know I always knew about what we might call Marty's other life, and I always knew when he was off on a little expedition. I also knew something of the way he worked. He almost never took anything but cash and he always stuck to a rigid code: he never stole from anyone unless he felt that they deserved it. And when he did get cash, I knew all about it." Tracy made to interrupt, but Mary shushed her and continued. "I know these can only have come from George Godwin, everything before that was accounted for. Marty developed a strong dislike for that man and so, knowing him, I think he made an exception and took these because he thought Godwin didn't deserve to have them. Marty knew Godwin must have stolen them, but he had no code at all and would have stolen them from someone who didn't deserve to lose them. Do you see?"

Tracy nodded, she found she saw it as in no way surprising that Marty took that attitude.

"That sounds just like the Marty I knew, though of course I didn't know the half of it until the last few days."

"Right, and there's something else in that case, I believe Marty must have stashed the jewels there temporally just until he could discover where Godwin had got them from. I'm sure he was going to try to find that out and then return them. Yes, I'm sure that's what he planned to do." Again the logic of this seemed to Tracy to fit in with all she now knew about Marty. Mary paused for a long moment and then added: "Now it's down to us, and that means we have to find out who the owner is and get these back to their proper home."

Chapter Thirty

In danger of becoming boss eyed

"If this is to be done I presume it has to be done in secret," said Jim who was now discussing the implications of the jewels' return with Tracy. "You can't just take the bag into a police station, hand it over and say you found it, right? Imagine how many awkward questions that would prompt." He and Tracy were discussing just how to respond to Mary's request, one which she had given with a clear indication that they should regard it as more akin to an instruction than a request.

"Yes, we all link back to Marty and that would immediately cause suspicion. If we admitted Marty stole them, but we said we don't know where from, the police might well investigate and ask more about other thefts he might have carried out and wonder if there was more to find. And I don't think Mary wants any more about his secret life known to all and sundry. It's a puzzle to know quite what to do."

"Maybe we could just post a package to the police?" Jim suggested.

"I don't think that would guarantee it got back to the rightful owner and that's what Mary wants. She wants to be sure. We'll have to give it some more thought." Besides Tracy's recent encounters with the late Constable Short did not give her great confidence in the trustworthiness of the police.

The answer to where the jewels came from lay, of course, on the internet. Jim suggested it and Tracy was happy for him to lead as he was more practiced in such a search than she was. The problem with the internet, as they both discovered with one look at the screen was that it was mind bogglingly extensive, putting something like 'Stolen jewellery' or 'Lost jewellery' into the likes of Google produced thousands and thousands of hits from all round the world and most seemed to be more individual, a photo of a lost engagement ring for instance.

"Let's think about it," said Jim. They were at Jim's place, there had just been a knock at the door and a take-away was delivered from the local Chinese. Tracy spread the boxes out on the kitchen table, added a couple of plates, and Jim poured them both a lager. They began to eat.

"Let's assume Godwin stole this stuff in the reth...ent pathtt," Jim struggled to continue to speak through a mouthful of crispy duck; once he had swallowed he went on. "He probably didn't hold onto this sort of stuff for very long and would want to turn items like this into cash. As far as we know he didn't have a wife or girlfriend to give the odd thing like this to. There's quite a bit of it too. Anyway, I think we could assume for the moment that it all comes from the same place and limit the search to recent thefts of collections of jewellery in this country."

"Sounds reasonable." Tracy stood up from the table. "What should I type in then?"

"Wait a bit, I don't want those sticky fingers of yours all over my computer, let's wait a moment." They finished eating and then Jim declared he would do it and sat down at his laptop, which he had sitting over on a side table. He entered "Stolen jewellery collection" and pressed Enter; a long list appeared. Jim refined his search and limited it by time. It still seemed to be a long list with, for the most part, each link beginning with a small amount of text and some pictures. Some involved high profile people, the name of more than one film star and celebrity appeared. Tracy had pointed out that the most distinctive of the items was a large and impressive diamond broach. The jewels were secure in their hiding place for the moment, but Tracy had taken a picture of the broach and of the whole collection on her phone to help them check, but they saw nothing that looked anything like it. They searched on, in danger of becoming boss eyed until, just when they were on the point of giving up, Tracy shouted out.

"Go back, go back." Jim retraced their electronic steps by a few clicks until she added: "Stop. There, I think that might be it." She held her phone up alongside the computer screen and said "Yes, I'm pretty sure that's it, what do you think?"

"Yes, I'm no jewellery expert but that looks right to me."

The broach was at the centre of a picture of jewellery stolen from a small stately home a couple of months back. Jim clicked on a link and was taken to a story in a local newspaper. Under the headline: *Elderly woman hurt as jewels stolen in raid on Bunting Hall,* the story told of an armed robbery. The place was described as being open to the public. Later Jim found it had a visitors' website and there they saw that it was just big enough to attract visitors. It was all rather small scale, a brief tour, free access to roam the gardens and tea and scones seemed to be about it.

The newspaper told how a masked man had broken into the place at night when the owner, a 'Rhona McDonald (72)' - newspapers always seem to point out someone's age - was alone in the house and in bed. She had been threatened with a pistol, dragged downstairs and forced to open a safe, then knocked unconscious as the intruder left. When she came round she phoned for help and was taken to hospital. The police investigated but the jewels had never been found though inquiries were stated as being 'ongoing', a phrase which Tracy suggested translated as 'long forgotten'. The police had called it a 'callous attack' and speculated that the attack had been carried out by a 'ruthless and professional criminal'. The jewels were family heirlooms, some of them hundreds of years old, and a few were due to have been auctioned soon after the robbery took place in what was described as a last ditch attempt to keep the old place going. Jim clicked on more links following the name of the Hall and found more recent stories about the consequences of the raid and the difficulties Rhona McDonald now faced as a result. Insurance of the jewels was reported to have been discontinued as being too high cost some years previously and now, without her selling some jewels as had been planned, the Hall was in increasing trouble and might well have to be sold.

"It looks like a match and the nature of the robbery sounds like Godwin alright, we know he was known to be ruthless, that poor woman's probably lucky to be alive," said Tracy, "Let's check the picture against the other items to be sure and then we can decide what to do next." She then sent Mary, who had asked to be kept informed without fail, a text: *Pretty sure we found its home. Talk later.* She was getting quite into the whole process of subterfuge and found that she found it was an automatic reflex not to use the word jewellery in the message. Jim, who had printed out all the pictures, was switching off the computer when Tracy asked him: "Hey, this is quite important. Where exactly is this place?"

"Well, it's a fair old way, it's in Scotland, somewhere near a place called Dunoon on the West coast. It seems that Godwin must have operated nationally." He did indeed and if they had checked further they would have discovered that there were several other robberies in the same area within days of the incident at Bunting Hall, all doubtless carried out as Godwin wanted to make his trip up north worthwhile. They wondered how he had identified his targets, but it was somewhat academic now the man was dead. However, the location did seem to complicate matters.

"It's not very convenient either, now we need to work out how to get the items back home as it were. A conference with Mary is called for, I think", she said, "I'm sure she'll reply to my message soon."

"Before we do anything else," Tracy said as she and Jim sat down in Mary's living room, "I must give you a bit of a catch up." Mary nodded as she fussed about with a tray of hot drinks, she had brought into the room with them; it was clear that no gathering in her house was complete without them.

"This has become very much a joint effort. I didn't go into it before, but I was having great trouble getting into the safe, and it was Jim who found the clue Marty had left linked to the combination, and it was him figured out what it meant too so that we could open it up. I'm not sure I would ever have got it on my own. We reckon Marty had always thought that one day something might make it necessary for him to pass on the information and he planned accordingly."

"I think you're right, sounds to me exactly like what he would do." Said Mary.

"One more thing, you asked the other day if Jim and I were an item, well we've decided we very much are," she turned and exchanged smiles with him, "we intend to move in together, so can we do this all of us now please?" Jim's smile remained as he took in the word 'intend'.

Mary smiled now too. "That's very good news and, yes, I'm sure we can. So where is this Bunting Hall place you've discovered then?" When they told her, she just smiled.
"I haven't been to Scotland for so many years, maybe a trip is in order, but first a phone call I think." Jim looked horrified.

"You can't just phone up, this has to be done without anyone else knowing about it, right?" he said, his comment

greeted by nods. "We'll need to get ourselves a burner phone."
Mary looked mystified and asked him to explain what that was.

Chapter Thirty-One

Only one way to do this properly

Though Mary helped out regularly on a stall in the market, Tracy had always thought of her as an old school traditional wife, staying at home while her husband went out to work, twice in a manner of speaking given his two 'jobs', and cooking roast lunches of the type that she and Jim had enjoyed with her recently. She thought of her as... well, mild was the word that came to mind, but the situation they were in had already showed her that she had misjudged her somewhat. Mary now took charge. Jim had explained what a burner phone was, that it meant that any call made on it couldn't be traced, and they now had one on hand ready to go. Tracy had looked up the number for Bunting Hall, which was listed on the website for the house, and a call was about to be made on the burner phone Jim had set up. It was evening and the three of them were gathered in the living room at Mary's home, this time with tea replaced by glasses of wine.

"What exactly are you going to say?" Tracy asked Mary.

"Well, it doesn't seem very complicated, we want to verify that we have the right jewellery, that it does come from Bunting Hall and that it's still missing. If it's not we know we're wrong. If it is, we need to arrange to get our find back to her as quickly as possible. It would be nice to know we are in time too, that she can still raise the money she needs to save the old place." Mary was very business-like and added: "SLAP, right?" Tracy was brought up short, she well knew what SLAP meant but it was not something she expected Mary to come out with.

"Okay, sounds like a plan indeed, how about the actual return, if everything checks out how do you think that should be done – a courier service, perhaps?"

"Well, first things first, eh, let's see how it goes... though I'm not very sure I would trust a courier. I do rather share Marty's careful nature you know." She dialled the number. It seemed to ring for a long time and Mary put her hand over the phone and said: "Big house, I expect." However, before much longer the phone was answered.

"Hello. Bunting Hall." Mary drew a breath and started to speak.

"Hello, is that Rhona McDonald?"

"That's right, who is it calling?" The woman's voice had a soft Scottish accent and sounded well educated.

"I think I have good news for you, may I call you Rhona?"

"No, you may not, who is this?" The tone was abrupt, and Mary felt she was not getting off to a good start.

"I can't tell you my name Mrs McDonald, but you'll love what I have to say, it's..." At this point there was an immediate interruption: "I don't buy anything on the phone, ever, go away whoever you are. You people are a pest."

With no further ado she hung up. Mary sat listening to the dialling tone for a moment or two then said with a hint of amusement in her voice:

"Apparently I'm a pest. She thought I was trying to sell her something." She recounted the conversation to the others and then dialled again, this time following Jim's suggestion to put the call on speaker so that they could all hear both sides of whatever was now said. The phone was answered within seconds this time and Mary jumped right in; she did not intend to be cut off again.

"Me again. Straight to it. I think I've found your stolen jewellery." There was what they all imagined to be a stunned silence for a moment at the other end, then just one word.

"What?" The anger had gone from the voice, which now had a slight tremble to it.

"Please listen, I don't think we got off on the right foot a moment ago, my apologies and I know I'm ringing out of the blue, but it's true, I think I've found your stolen jewellery."

"I can't believe it. How? Who on Earth are you?"

"No names I'm afraid, because of the way I came across this I can't say, I might get myself and others into trouble. But I would assure you I am in no way connected to the thief and I am certainly not the thief myself: I don't own a gun, I've never been to Dunoon in my life… and anyway I'm not a man. Also I do want you to have the jewels back, is there still time to raise the money you need?"

"Yes, I think so, yes there would be."

"Okay forgive me but we need to be sure. I need to be sure. Tell me, do you use email?"

"Yes, I do, why?"

"So that you can send me a picture of what you lost. I have pictures from the press, we found that by searching online, but it would be good to have something clearer and which comes direct from you. First may I ask you to describe what happened, the robbery that is? Tell me a bit about it."

Rhona McDonald agreed and launched into what sounded like a well-rehearsed spiel; she doubtless had been through it many times with the police and others in the aftermath of the crime. She described how she had been sound asleep in bed, the first she knew of an intruder was when she was shaken awake and then was roughly dragged out of bed and down the stairs. She later discovered the man had broken in by smashing a French window and had found the safe behind a picture in the study. She said she had been made to disclose the safe's combination number and did so as she was terrified and in fear of her life. Once the intruder had the safe open, he had hit her. She never saw his face and knew nothing of what happened next, she managed to phone for help after she came round a little later and the next she knew she was in hospital. She spent several days there while the doctors checked her out in case, she had concussion.

"It must have been a dreadful experience, I'm so sorry." Mary sympathised. Next, she asked about the jewels and Rhona explained.

"They are from my father's family, have been in it over many generations and are reputed to date from the time of Bonnie Prince Charlie. Frankly they are one of the few things really worth seeing in the house when people visit, although many come for the gardens, they're magnificent. My gardener is a miracle worker. Sorry, you don't want to know that, I'm sure." Mary nodded to the others, a so far so good signal, as she replied.

"Well, I'm sure now that I'm speaking to the right person, so once you have emailed me a picture, we can decide what we can do next to get them back to you. Can you do that for me?" The question was answered with a promise to do just that and Mary read out an email address that Jim had organised to go with the new phone she now knew as a burner, they ended the conversation and a few minutes later a picture arrived. She had ended the conversation by saying that she would ring back in a day or two and stressing that Rhona should talk to no one about the conversation or 'it might jeopardise the whole thing'. Mary got them all to cluster round the picture.

"I don't think there's any doubt, do you, we've tracked them down, so now what?" Tracy posed the question to Mary. They all agreed that they had matched the jewels to their rightful owner and discussed the best method to get them home again. Registered post was laughed out of court in an instant and Mary remained with a deep suspicion of any courier saying that she did not propose to make a present of them to 'some guy in a crash helmet'. They went round the houses for a bit and then Mary laid down the law.

"There's only one proper way to do this, we deliver them," she said. "I would like to see the place and also see the look on Rhona's face when she gets them back." Jim took on the practical role.

"You do remember where she lives don't you?" he said, but Mary was adamant: "Yes, it's a long way, train to Glasgow, I think, and then a hire car. Time consuming but no big problem. Well, it's nice to have that settled. Now that's out the way who's for a cup of tea… I think the wine's finished? Last one before bed."

The kettle was boiled and tea was duly made, Mary found biscuits, chocolate digestives which she declared were always Marty's favourite, adding that was true only provided the covering was dark chocolate. They all let everything sink in, Tracy and Jim were left wondering about it all, but Mary seemed to have no outstanding questions and insisted that the matter was as good as done and dusted. Despite reservation about the plan to visit Scotland, Tracy found that she could think of nothing that would have any chance of succeeding in getting Mary to change her mind, besides she could think of no satisfactory alternative guaranteed to return the jewels to their owner.

"Well if you're sure Mary, you can't possibly go on your own though, we need to find a time when we can all do it. And there's arrangements to be made, train tickets to book – and seats, I'm not standing all that way – a car to hire, hotel rooms to reserve, it's not a journey that can be done there and back in a day."

"Alright my dear, if you two will come too that will be wonderful. Thank you. We'll set a date, then I will make all the arrangements. I'll pay all the costs too, don't you worry about that." Her promise to pay made Tracy think of the money sitting in the safe under the Jowett car in Marty's lock up; nothing had been discussed about that yet – and it would be sufficient to buy a great deal more than three train tickets. Tracy checked that Jim was also up for the trip and found they were all agreed.

"Now one more thing before you go." Mary held up a hand as she spoke. "There's a gap in what you told me about the lock up, what was this clue that Marty left?"

"Jim worked it out, he should tell you." Tracy said and in due course Jim was pleased to find Mary congratulating him on his puzzling out abilities as she put it.

Chapter Thirty-Two

A Scottish speciality

Mary was as good as her word and a few days later, after a little conferring about dates, Tracy received a text that confirmed the matter:

```
All   arrangements   made,   tickets   booked   for
Saturday week.
```

Mary was very much in the driving seat on the matter of returning the jewels, and her conviction about it needing to be done and done in person was unshakeable. Tracy had spoken to her a number of times about it, trying to inject a note of caution into the arrangement. Mary had agreed, she did, as she had said, share Marty's careful nature. Tracy had made three specific suggestions, in the main in the light of a fear that Rhona McDonald might tell the local police about what was happening. First, it was agreed that one of them should go to the house alone and then only then after they had observed the place for a while ahead of that. Secondly, that Mary, who insisted on being the one to go, should disguise herself and thirdly that Rhona McDonald should not be told about the visit until the last minute; though of course, she had no idea where Mary came from or who she was.

Mary telephone Bunting Hall again in light of their discussions. When Rhona answered she expressed relief at their renewed contact.

"I'm so pleased to hear from you again, I've spent the last few days wondering if all this was a dream or just some cruel practical joke."

"It's no joke Rhona, may I call you that? I believe the only safe way to do this is to hand the jewels over to you myself. I need to fix to visit you, however – and forgive me, you sound like a nice lady, but so that I can't be surprised by walking into the arms of a policeman, I'm going to tell you a week. On one of the days in that week I'll call you again literally as I approach your front door. I don't believe the police will camp out at your place for a week so I'm hoping that will be safe." Mary quoted her dates with the day they intended to make the visit lurking unidentified in the middle of the period she quoted.

"That's fine, but, I have to ask, is there something you want in return, is this some sort of ransom?"

Rhona had been thinking and had come up with a worry. Mary reassured her, saying that her one intention was to get the jewels back to their rightful owner.

"Thank you, I'm so grateful and I assure you I won't tell a soul. I suspect that if the police were to be involved then I wouldn't see the jewels for ages. By then it might be too late, I have to repay a loan and get this place back on an even keel."

With the arrangement made Mary ended the call following Rhona offering renewed thanks for what was about to happen.

Mary and Tracy kept in touch over the following few days and when Tracy called in one evening the door was opened by a stranger. The woman was blond, had a low hung fringe, was wearing heavy horned rimmed spectacles and had the ruddy cheeks of an inveterate drinker. For a second or two Tracy wondered who this was then, as realisation dawned, the figure spoke up.

"How do you like my disguise?" said Mary making Tracy laugh out loud.

"I hope you won't mind me saying this Mary, but it's… well it's a bit over the top, and by a bit I mean a lot." Mary turned and looked in the hall mirror, finding no fault.

"So, what do you suggest?" She asked. An hour or so later they had found a compromise that both found acceptable and one more bit of the plan fell into place.

The time seemed to fly by and soon the day of their travel dawned, the three conspirators got a taxi to King's Cross Station and settled in on the train for their journey. Mary had organised a picnic, which they ate mid-way to Scotland and made a joke of the fact that it included Scotch eggs. Mary read a book, Tracy had brought a number of magazines and Jim busied himself on his phone. They talked little and avoided saying anything about the plan and what they were going to do for fear of being overheard. In the latter part of the journey the scenery showed they were over the border and once the train pulled into the station in Glasgow they disembarked and went to the office of the car hire company with which Mary had made the rental booking. Tracy was to be the nominated driver as they were not driving a great enough distance to need to share that load and their plan meant that both Mary and Jim would have other duties.

They set off, the sat nav in the car (Mary had insisted on this being included in the rental arrangement) guiding them out of a city with which none of them were familiar. The majority of the buildings they passed were grey granite and made their surroundings seem somewhat alien. With the city left behind they were soon on the road towards Gourock to the West with the view opening up and the Firth of Clyde, a wide stretch of water visible on their right hand side. The way to Dunoon involved crossing the Clyde via The Caledonian MacBrayne ferry– CalMac as the locals called it - and Jim checked the timetable on his phone as they got closer.

"Not bad," he said as Tracy drove into the town and signs appeared directing people to the ferry embarkation point, "we're in luck, there's one leaving in fifteen minutes." In due course the car was sitting on the flat deck of the ferry. They did not get out.

"Stay put please," Mary had said, "the fewer people that see us the better." In truth there was nothing to distinguish them amongst the other cars and passengers on the trip and they felt safe enough. Being a rental the car had a local number plate, which would draw no attention and the ferry crew member who came round to each vehicle collecting payment hardly glanced at them. They had set off first thing, the main train journey had taken just short of five hours and after half an hour or so on board they disembarked from the ferry at the pier in the middle of the town and located and checked into the hotel Mary had booked, which overlooked the water. By the time they were booked in it was late afternoon.

"Right, time to check this Bunting Hall place out," said Mary, once they had dropped their bags in their rooms and assembled again in the hotel reception area. They returned to the car and Tracy drove them out of the small town and along the coast road heading west.

"The views are lovely," said Mary, "they have been since soon after we left Glasgow, so very different from home, it's a pity we can't stay longer and explore."

They found Bunting Hall without any trouble, a few miles out of Dunoon the road turned to the right as it followed the coast northwards and a few miles further on they saw the place appear high above the road on their right-hand side. A gate at the end of the drive stood open and a sign on it confirmed that they were in the right place. Mary was still concentrating on the views and commented on how houses way back had been able to pick their sites unhindered by planning laws and that up here having a stunning view seemed to be a priority. They drove on past the entrance, alongside which was a larger notice about visiting, and Tracy turned the car round and stopped.

"You're up now, Jim." She said. The plan was for Jim, who was dressed for walking, to have a good look round in case the place appeared to be being watched. He got out of the car and Tracy told him they would pick him up in an hour at the same spot. They drove back the way they can come and turned right along a side road that took them to Toward Point Lighthouse. They parked and had a bit of a wander to give Jim time. The small lighthouse appeared deserted and Mary said she thought that if it was still used it must be automated.

"Lovely views though; that must be the island of Bute over there," she added, pointing out over the water. They chatted a bit, just whiling away time as Jim checked things out and then Tracy drove back the way they had come to pick him up and then she headed back towards the hotel. As Tracy drove back along the coast road towards the hotel he reported back.

"I didn't go too close to the house, which is a pretty impressive place by the way, but I walked right round it, there's a footpath along one side of the grounds, and just empty hillside beyond, the gardens are beautiful and the whole area was quiet, I saw no one and no sign of a police car. I think Rhona has been as good as her word, there's no sign that she's told anyone about this. I saw no evidence of anyone watching out for our handover. It's no guarantee, of course, but I think we can be confident about tomorrow going to plan." Both Tracy and Mary reckoned he was right, but it was an odd thing that they were doing and if they were discovered it would at the very least raise some awkward questions. Back at the hotel they ate dinner together in the restaurant and retired to their respective rooms having agreed to meet for breakfast at 8.00 a.m.

The morning was cloudy and dry, but the view from the dining room was still striking; more so for people living in a big city.

"What's an Arbroath Smokie?" Jim was finding the menu listed some oddities and asked the question. None of them knew the answer and Tracy asked the waitress to be told it was a Scottish speciality, a kind of smoked haddock. She was tempted to try it, but the others all urged her to go for something simpler. Nevertheless they all enjoyed a cooked breakfast, after which Mary settled their bills and, bags packed away in the boot, they headed off for Bunting Hall again; this time for Mary to go in and meet Rhona. Mary, who had insisted all along that she be the one to make the handover, was wearing a headscarf that rendered her hair colour and style invisible and had kept the large horned rimmed spectacles she had tested out on Tracy a few days earlier. They were a pair she had chosen some years back and never liked or used. A feeling had been expressed that they were being a bit paranoid, but the plan remained for Mary to go up to the house on her own. She had the burner phone to call them when she was ready to be picked up again. Tracy didn't drive up the drive to prevent Mary's arrival being obviously linked to any particular car or other people. She stopped on the road near the entrance to drop Mary off, there was little other traffic around, it was a Sunday morning and still early, all was quiet.

"She promised to stay in over these days until my visit, so I think we can be sure she'll be there. She's very keen to get this stuff back after all. I just hope no one else is there. Okay, off I go." She got out of the car, headed up the drive and within a few steps was hidden by the huge rhododendrons growing on either side of it. Tracy put the car into gear and drove on heading further away from the town.

"Fingers crossed," said Jim.

Mary paused half way to the house and made the promised phone call to announce her arrival. Once Rhona answered she pitched straight in, succinct and to the point.

"Rhona, you're expecting me. I'm walking up your drive right now, please be ready to let me in." She clicked the phone off without waiting for a reply, and a few minutes later she reached the front door of the grand looking stone house, it was a massive and ancient piece of oak set between two round stone pillars and which looked like it had been in service for very many years. She went up a couple of steps and rang the bell, pulling on a large traditional bell pull set in the wall. She could hear a distant ringing as she did so and after only a few seconds had passed the door was opened; Rhona had complied with her request and been nearby and ready. The woman who stood at the door was seventy two years old, Mary knew that from the internet, she had grey hair but was a sprightly looking lady wearing a tweed suit and with an apron clutched in her hand which, in all likelihood she had taken off as she walked to the door. The thought of the television programme *To the manor born* flashed into Mary's mind, Rhona looked the part; she just seemed to belong in such a setting.

"Good morning." Rhona seemed uncertain what else to say for a second, as did Mary, who just waited for her to continue.

"Thank you for being here. Come away in." Mary recognised the voice as having the same Scottish burr she had heard on the phone, there was no doubt this was the same person she had spoken to on the phone. At that moment Mary found that she hadn't thought this bit of their plan through in any real detail. She wondered: should she just handover the velvet bag and leave or what? However, faced with a woman who looked like the very antithesis of a threat she decided to accept the invitation. She stepped into the house, finding herself in an imposing hall from which a long curved staircase swept up to the upper levels, and being told that the kettle was on and that she should sit down in the living room while Rhona organised refreshments. Already this was taking longer than she thought, but having decided to come inside she accepted the invitation, went into the room indicated and sat down on a large sofa. It seemed longer but Rhona was back in just two or three minutes with a tray. She laid things out on a side table, sat down at the other end of the sofa and once that was done she spoke.

"This may be an unexpected and unusual meeting, but this is Scotland; so of course, I have scones." The situation seemed bizarre and surreal and Mary found she could not repress a smile.

"It certainly is… and thank you." Rhona checked how she liked her tea, poured for them both from a silver teapot and handed Mary a cup. She thought that in all probability the china must be as old as the jewellery. They both sat looking at each other and over Rhona's shoulder Mary could see a vista of water and hills stretching into the distance beyond the garden she had just walked through as she faced the large window in a very traditionally furnished sitting room. The sofa and chairs were tartan covered, there were pictures on the walls of hills, lochs, sheep and stags and one could well imagine it was a room that had been home to the serving of scones over many, many years. Mary calculated that the room was almost as large as most of the downstairs of her house, she opened her bag and was about to begin the handover and tell Rhona the little she was prepared to say, when Rhona beat her to it and spoke first.

"I still don't know what to call you, but I have to tell you that I did speak to the police."

Chapter Thirty-Three

Hope you didn't worry

Tracy had driven a few miles further up the road to a spot where she could turn the car and then pull off the road, the tyres crunched on loose granite stones and she pulled on the brake and turned off the engine. She and Jim sat in silence for a few moments, for Londoners the silence around them in such a location seemed almost palpable; a seagull swooped low over the car and glided on out over the water. The spell was broken a moment later as Jim spoke up.

"Do you reckon we should be worried?" They both declared it was a pretty weird thing to be doing, so they both wondered how matters might turn out, but Tracy was determined to be positive.

"Well, it all seemed fine, it has done all the way through. Mary said that if the worst came to the worst and the police are there she'll just say she found the jewels in Marty's sock drawer and there would be no way anyone could think she stole them. Or us. The police know Marty was at Godwin's house so getting them to believe that he was the original thief should be no problem, but… anyway, let's not worry, I'm sure it will all be fine. Come on, let's talk about something else - and keep that phone handy, eh, she'll be calling before you know it. We can be back to the gate in three or four minutes if I put my foot down."

Mary was both shocked and surprised by Rhona's mention of the police. She had convinced herself the handover could be made without any problem and, more important, she had convinced herself that this was the right thing to do. She had always approved of Marty's code and she wanted nothing more than to get the jewels back to their rightful home, more so having discovered how important they were to this old house and its elderly owner. For a moment she was dumbstruck, a flash of fear made her look around her eyes drawn to the single door. Rhona took in her frightened expression and went on at once.

"Oh, sorry, I can see you're horrified, please don't be; there are no police here and there are not going to be any. To be honest they were not much interested, though they gave me a number to call and said they could be here in ten minutes if I should need them. I'm not altogether sure that they believed me.

It was just that, after we spoke on the telephone, I felt that if you were not what you said you were, then I might be in some danger. I got quite a knock on the head during the robbery, you know, and I can assure you that such an event does rather leave one feeling a trifle insecure. Anyway you do seem to be what you say, in fact I can't imagine anyone looking less like a gangster, so stop worrying and help yourself to a scone. The jam's made from strawberries from the garden, you know – and it's very good, though I do say so myself." Mary remained mute, none of this was what she had expected, but she managed to focus again on what she was wanting to say.

"Okaaay... I guess. Anyway, let's get to it shall we." She opened her bag and retrieved the black velvet bag. She held it up and then opened the drawer string, she leaned forward and tipped the contents onto the sofa next to her host a move with which she took great care. "Are these yours or have I had a wasted journey?"

Rhona stared at the untidy pile of jewellery, she reached forward, and with some care she used a single finger to spread them apart so that each individual item was visible and then picked up the broach, which sparkled in the light as she moved it. Her face lit up as she did this and she smiled a broad smile while she turned it this way and that making the stones catch the light.

"Oh my goodness, I never thought I would see these again, the police said to forget it, they thought they were gone forever, and yes, they are mine... and every single item seems to be here. I really can't thank you enough. I don't know how you came to find them – and I don't need to know I suppose – but most people would not have done what you have, you're a good person."

"Well, I'm not sure about that, though I was sure, I am sure, that this is the right thing to do."

"Yes, yes indeed, thank you so much. Now listen, if I sell a few of these to pay off this wretched loan, their return is certain to become public, I hope that's alright. I don't know who you are or where you're from, well I presume from below the border somewhere, but I don't even know your name. If asked I propose saying that the bag was left in the post box at the front door, so that said there would be nothing more I could ever be expected to add. Does that seem suitable?"

"Yes, that seems a very good solution – and it occurs to me that the story of their return might get you some good publicity too, encourage more visitors to come here perhaps. Now do tell me about the house, I need to shut up for a minute and eat this lovely scone."

Down the road Tracy and Jim had tracked a full hour going by with no word from Mary. Now both of them had started to worry, the view was wasted on them and they were both trying to decide how long to leave things.

"Surely it should have taken only a few minutes to hand over the bag, what do you think's going on? Is Mary okay?" It was Jim's turn to speak along the lines that they had both been taking for more than half an hour. As before Tracy just kept saying every version of 'I don't know', 'I don't know what to do for the best' and 'what do you think?' But now, when they were both thinking that a whole sixty minutes had passed since they dropped Mary off at the house, they had both decided that it had now been far too long and that some action was therefore called for.

"We can't just sit here, we have to go back to the house, one of us has to go in and see what's happening," said Tracy, but before Jim could reply and before they could get to debating who should do what and how, Tracy's mobile rang. Despite having spent more than an hour waiting for that very sound she was startled by it, she scrabbled and fumbled as she strove to answer it fast and, once there, she put it on speaker so that Jim too could hear everything that was said. It turned out to be very little.

"Hello there, I'll be at the bottom of the drive in five minutes, everything's fine. I hope you didn't worry." Mary did not wait for a reply and ended the call, she was too busy giving Rhona a hug as they said goodbye. Tracy and Jim looked at each other and, in unison, they heaved sighs of relief.

"I'll give her 'hope you didn't worry' so I will," said Tracy with feeling as she started the engine and slipped the car into gear. In a few minutes they approached the drive and could see Mary already emerging onto the road. She had taken off her headscarf and the huge glasses when she reached the road and flashed them a broad smile as they pulled up. As the car door slammed shut behind her Tracy drove off, she did not want to remain in the area any longer than necessary. As she concentrated on her driving Jim asked the question.

"So, what happened… and why did it take so long? And yes, you had us worried, *really* worried." Tracy glanced in the mirror as the question was asked; Mary was still smiling.

"Sorry, it did take a little longer than I thought, but then Rhona had spoken to the police." Tracy swerved to the left and hit the brakes as she pulled the car into the kerb and stopped.

"What?" She almost shouted the words.

"Oh, I'm sorry dear, I couldn't resist it. It's true, but everything worked out fine, let me explain. No more shocks Tracy, I'm sorry, so you can drive on now. Let's get to a ferry shall we. I'm sure Scotland's lovely, but I still can't wait to get back home to London." As Tracy drove on she then told them about her meeting: Rhona's admission of her fear of being in danger, her talking to the police, their seeming lack of interest, her decision not to call them when she met Mary and found the proposition was real, and her joy at seeing the jewels again.

"It was worth all this hassle just to see her face," Mary went on. "She's such a nice lady. She'd made the two of us scones, would you believe it? And home-made jam, that added some time, it would have been rude not to try one and they were delicious; I considered asking for a couple to bring for you two, but I thought it better for her to assume I was on my own. Sorry about that. After scones we set off on a tour of the house. It really is a beautiful place and it's so… well, it's so Scottish. There's tartan everywhere and swords and so on hung on the walls. There was a stag's head with huge antlers in pride of place over a huge open fireplace in the living room. The house will be safe now too. I'm so sorry if I worried you, but I said it was the right thing to do and I'm even surer of that now. It very much was. You know Rhona's someone I could be good friends with, though, don't worry, I'm not going back for a weekend break. I stuck to the plan and disclosed nothing. She still doesn't even know my name and has no idea where I live or how I came to have her jewels; I just sort of implied that it involved a long, complicated chain of events, which is pretty much the truth. Anyway, I owe you two a huge vote of thanks, I would have hated trying to do this all on my own. Now what time's the next ferry, do you think?" She rummaged in her bag for the timetable they had picked up on their earlier crossing leaving Jim and Tracy pleased and relieved in equal measure as they struggled for something to say in response.

"Well done you then," Tracy said after a moment. "Just please don't get us that worried ever again, right."

Back at the pier Tracy drove into the line of vehicles queuing for the next ferry sailing to Gourock with a mere couple of minutes to spare. They watched the cars ahead of them move forward and the deck filling up and wondered if there would be space for them all; they were last but one on. With their job safely done this time once on board all three of them got out of the car and stood at a rail looking across the water to the hills as Dunoon fell behind in the ship's wake.

"You know there's one loose end," Jim told them, and he reached into his jacket pocket and held the burner phone out over the water churning past below them.

"Go for it," said Mary and Jim released his hold and the phone was gone, the splash of its falling lost and undetectable in the rush of water into which it fell. The act seemed to rule a line.

After the roller coaster of the last couple of hours they were all just grateful to relax and have it all finished. Mary found herself thinking of Marty. She reckoned he would have been well pleased, she reckoned she had done him proud. They relaxed as the journey got under way. There was no picnic on the train this time so Jim was given some cash by Mary, who was still insisting on paying all the costs of the trip, and sent along to the buffet car. They all relaxed more and more as the journey progressed, though at one point a family with two rambunctious young children came into the carriage after having boarded at an intermediate station stop, for a moment it looked as if peace had gone for the duration, but they disappeared out of the carriage at the other end heading, according to the mother, for the buffet car.

The one slight distraction thereafter was two grumpy old men a few rows away putting the world to rights as they pointed out the regrettable and surprising lack of common sense in those organising everything from the railways to retailers ... *no wonder so many people shop online...* and doing so with a particular concern for the British Government. They all dozed a bit and, journey over, they got a taxi at King's Cross and made the first stop dropping Mary off at her house. She stood at the window of the cab for a moment before she turned and went to her front door.

"My thanks to you both, now keep in touch, there's other things we need to sort out Tracy. About the shop, that is. Speak soon. Good night." It was true that there were some things remaining to be finalised about the running of the shop, but Tracy guessed that was not all that Mary was talking about. She turned to Jim.

"I reckon she means the money," she said, thinking of the considerable pile of bank notes that remained locked away in Marty's secret safe.

Chapter Thirty-Four

The matter of the money

The next few days that followed the successful trip to Scotland were busy ones. Tracy had had to close the shop on the Saturday and that was very often a busy day for key cutting and the like as people themselves at work during the week came into the shop. Doing so seemed to have made the next open day busier, after all a new key is often needed with some urgency. She was behind on her paperwork too and, all in all it began to make her think that she was in need of some sort of assistant. What with one thing and another, it was a while before she was able to speak with Mary again. Then when she had phoned and proposed getting together, Mary had delayed setting any meeting by asking her and Jim to come to lunch again a day or two later on the coming Sunday.

"Okay, that would be great, if you are sure you are up to it, you must be missing Marty so much," said Tracy when they had spoken on the phone. She found that it was difficult to know just how to talk about Marty but she felt she should. Mary assured here she was fine and still found things easier if she kept herself busy. Before the call ended Tracy added: "Jim too?"

"Yes, of course, though there is a little paperwork we must go through after lunch as I think I have everything sorted about the shop now. Marty would have wanted all that arranged promptly, you know." They agreed a time and later Tracy pre-warned Jim about shop discussions that would be part of the occasion, promising him that would take but a few moments.

After lunch on Sunday, for which Mary had again cooked a roast, a chicken this time followed by treacle tart and custard, they sat around the table with cups of coffee and Mary became business-like.

"Okay, things to say, things to sort out," she said. "First off Tracy, about the shop. I think it's all very straightforward, with Marty gone, after considering it for a while I don't think I need any formal involvement. Not that I could ever help technically, of course, but if you need any advice about, I don't know, keeping the books or whatever, I'll always help if I can. So, the business should be in your sole name from now on."

"But what about sharing the income, I'm sure Marty would have wanted you to..." Tracy started to protest, but Mary cut her off.

"No, he and I discussed it a while before your year of working was due to come up. He wanted you to take over the shop, not completely then of course, but he planned to retire bit by bit starting after he hit sixty, to do less and have time for other things, well... now that's not possible it seems logical – right – to move straight on to it being your business. He was very proud of you, you know. He took a chance with you though, you know that too, you were – dare I say it – not the most obvious prospect at the time and I must confess I told him it might all end in tears, but he insisted. He was right too, you've done him proud, though I have to say that he reckoned it was in large part down to his training role, any assistants he'd employed in the shop before were not working with him and understudying him as you have been." At this point Tracy tried to interrupt but Mary shushed her.

"I was wrong, you have so done him proud and look at the way you've helped with this jewellery business – you too Jim, for that matter, I appreciate your help too – I'm more than happy to see you continue with the shop. Besides we never had kids, just didn't happen, and he wanted to see the business continue in some suitable way, to pass it on to someone who would appreciate it. Anyway, it's a done deal, right. I don't want any arguments. None." Tracy was pleased, but unsure what to say.

"Well, I'm delighted of course, thank you, thank you so much. Saying that seems so inadequate. Sorry, I'm just lost for words." Tracy paused then, after a moment's thought, went on. "Oh, one thing, despite that the name still definitely stays: it will be Holmes & Hines over the door, the sign painting's booked in as planned and is due to be done very soon."

"I appreciate that. There's something else you might help with if you've a mind, the two of you that is." Jim, who had remained silent while the shop had been discussed now looked up.

"What's that?" he asked.

"It's the car, the Jowett or whatever the old banger is called. I know it was Marty's pride and joy, but as you know he never kept those cars for long once the renovation work was completed and he was satisfied with it, so it needs to be sold. I have our trusty Golf and I think the Jowett needs to go to an enthusiast, someone who knows how to keep it up. Can you help with that?"

"Yes, of course," said Jim. "There must be specialist websites for the likes of that, I can check it out. And get some sort of idea of value too."

"Oh, I know that," Mary chipped in at once. "Marty was about ready to sell. He told me he wanted to get around £10,000 for it, close to that anyway. Maybe we should ask, say, £9950 for it, though you might need to negotiate and accept a little less, I fancy Marty's pride in his work might have inflated his valuation a bit. One other thing: before you get anyone coming round to see the car and wanting a test drive, you should give it a go. It's not like driving something modern, the gear change is on the steering column, there's no power steering and…" Mary saw Tracy grinning and stopped in mid-sentence.

"What?"

"Sorry. Nothing. I just didn't think you were so knowledgeable about cars, that's all." It was then Mary's turn to grin.

"Well you knew Marty, he was passionate about his renovation projects, I couldn't *avoid* gathering a bit of information about them along the way even if I tried, and believe me, I did try! I'll add both your names to the insurance so that you can drive it and I'll give you all the paperwork, though I'll no doubt need to sign something when a sale is made to make it legal. I'm the car's official owner, you know, it was arranged that way to keep it all separate from the locksmith business. Incidentally, once the car's gone from the lock up, that's yours to use too and I've put the van in your name too." Tracy looked to be on the point of interrupting again once the van was mentioned, but Mary stopped her with a few words.

"No argument, remember. The lock up was bought by Marty's father years ago, so I guess it's mine now. I am going to amend my will so that it ends up with you Tracy; it needs to stay linked to the shop. Not that the will matters for a while yet I hope."

"Well, that's very good of you too and, yes, not for a long while yet I'm sure."

Tracy marvelled at how Mary was managing to be so business-like in the circumstances, she was pleased there was something else they could do to help Mary and dealing with the sale of the car should be straightforward. She double checked with Jim that he didn't mind doing the donkey work and asked Mary what else there was to sort out. It was still not so long since Marty had passed away, Mary appeared to be coping well, the funeral arrangements had all gone off to everyone's satisfaction and her sister Betty staying for a while had helped, though she had since returned home, insisting Mary let her know if there was anything more she could do. Mary was still at the stage of being busy with things that had to be done in the aftermath of Marty's death and Tracy suspected that she would find things more difficult as that situation changed as time went by.

"What else do we need to discuss?" she asked.

"I think that's it for the moment, my thanks to you both, you've been a great help." Tracy noticed that there was no mention of the money Marty had taken from George Godwin; it was still locked away in the safe at the lock up. She decided to give Mary time and not to mention it for the moment. They left with Tracy bemused by developments and continuing to say that she did not know what to say.

Tracy and Jim went for a drive in the old Jowett a day or two later. Jim drove and it went well and, though Jim found that the gear change needed a bit of getting used to, he was confident he could drive it well enough to do what was necessary to get it sold. Some research online had him certain about price and he soon had its availability listed on what he hoped was an appropriate specialist website. After a while he began to get calls from potential buyers. Some who came to see it were nosey time wasters, enthusiasts who wanted to see the car, though all were complimentary about the standard of the renovation work Marty had done. Before too long an offer was made, some brief negotiation ensued and a deal was done. The guy was as much an enthusiast as Marty had been and just as difficult to deflect from lengthy discussions about every detail of the old car. Jim contacted Mary about the paperwork, a secure method of payment was arranged, and a few days later Jim met the purchaser at the lock up to open up and the car went on its way to its new home. With the deal complete and the money in Mary's bank account she sent a text to Jim:

`Thanks for all your help with the car. Much appreciated.`

She was still grieving, of course, but continued to find that she was getting some satisfaction from the process of sorting everything out. When Jim and Tracy spoke about his conversations with Mary, Tracy had one question.

"Did she mention the little matter of the money?" Tracy asked. Jim said not.

"No, not a word. It's not possible she's forgotten about it is it? We can't just leave it sitting there, I suppose I should raise it with her, but somehow doing that is awkward, though I don't understand why it should be." Jim agreed, saying that it was the solitary loose end outstanding from the whole affair.

Chapter Thirty-Five

Best said in private

When Tracy arrived at the shop a few days after the old car had been sold there were two ladders propped up against the outside wall and the sign writer, a local and an old friend of Marty's, who she had engaged was already at the top of one of them busy with the process of installing the planned new shop sign. He spotted Tracy opening the door below him and shouted down to her.

"Morning. I'm about done."

"You must have started at the crack of dawn," she retorted and paused for a moment stepping back to inspect his handiwork as he told her that the work was in the painting and that it then took a quick dozen screws to put it up on site.

"Well, it looks good, makes the place look a lot smarter and more up to date, do you want a cuppa, I'll put the kettle on." A few minutes later he was at the door brushing down the white boiler suit he wore and then he came into the shop.

"Tea or coffee, Andy?" she asked, then made him his preferred brew and they chatted for a few minutes as he drank it and she got herself organised for the day.

"Sad about Marty," he said as he left. "I'd been telling him he needed a smart new sign for more years that I can remember. Good luck with it all, keep up the good work, it's what he would have wanted. He was a good bloke." Another reminder of the way Marty was thought of by local people, she thought, wondering whether his good luck remark had meant the sign or her running the shop. As she fired up the computer, and with no customer having yet come into the shop to demand her attention, she took a moment to enter the name Bunting Hall into Google. It was a search she had done a few times since their trip to Scotland. A few clicks brought her to a new story in the local paper that covered the area around Dunoon, and she read a headline saying: *Stolen jewels mysteriously returned: Bunting Hall saved.* The story beneath told of Rhona McDonald finding an unexpected package in her post-box one morning and opening it to find all the missing jewellery intact and returned. She was quoted as saying: *It's all very mysterious, I suppose that there must be some good people left in the world, so a big thank you to my unknown benefactor. This will save the old house too, I was threatened with having to sell the place to repay a loan and, while I will be sad to see any of the jewels go, selling just a few will set us straight again.* The story also referred back to the break in and the theft as well as to Rhona being injured; it ended with the reporter saying that she seemed to have made a full recovery.

It was a story Tracy had been watching out for and she printed out copies of the page to show to Jim and Mary later. It gave her a rather good feeling too to think that their exploits and detective work had had such a useful result. It was a feeling she knew was shared by Mary and Jim. According to Mary, Rhona was a nice lady; she realised that she couldn't take the chance of keeping in touch with her but she wished her well. Thinking of the jewels made Tracy think back. It had been quite a year and recent events since the police had come calling on Marty had been something of a roller coaster. With George Godwin dead and gone there had been no further word from the police, who she suspected were pleased to see the back of him and had filed the matter away together with their disappointment at not nabbing a murderer. At 5.30 she was about to lock up and leave the shop when the bell on the door rang as someone entered; it was Mary.

Mary soon proved to be somewhat mysterious about things. She asked if Tracy was meeting Jim that evening and was told nothing was arranged. She then asked Tracy to meet her at the house later.

"Dress smartly please, we are going out," she looked Tracy up and down. "No jeans, I imagine you do have legs." Despite Tracy's protests and questions she would say no more about what she planned, just made it clear that she regarded the invitation as being mandatory. Once Tracy reached the house later, clad in her best dress and a jacket, a smartly dressed Mary came out to meet her and, almost at once, a cab drew up at the kerb. It had to have been booked because Mary just waved to the driver rather than give him any instructions and climbed in, Tracy joined her and the taxi headed west.

Once in the West End they were dropped off at, of all things, a casino. Mary would still say nothing other than, "Come on you, all will be revealed." Once inside Mary made Tracy wait and headed off to a counter. The place was busy, full of well-dressed people who looked as if they were not short of a bob or two. It was opulent: all marble and gilt, with high ceilings, it looked a little like the large public areas one sees in cruise ships. A clatter of slot machines could be heard from beyond some long velvet curtains. After a few minutes Mary returned with what seemed to Tracy like a huge pile of brightly coloured gambling chips; she could not imagine how much money it represented, but it was, she suspected, a good deal.

"Come on Mary, you're a dark horse, I didn't know you were into this sort of thing. What goes on? Are you having some sort of funny turn?"

"As I said, all will be revealed. Don't ask questions but you must do one thing for me, okay?" Tracy said she would. "Right, I need you to ring my mobile when I tell you. Keep your phone set up and ready, keep it hidden and just press the call button. Don't speak and just follow my lead. Okay?" The last word was said with considerable force, Tracy started to speak, but any words were cut off with a look, so she just nodded. She was learning a few new and surprising things about Mary of late, she thought, though what all this was about she as yet had no idea.

Tracy had never been in a casino before, she set up her phone as instructed as they walked along and was led to a roulette table where they found seats and Tracy watched in awe as Mary put a few of her chips on numbers and the wheel spun. She did this several times, speaking to Tracy as she did so and even asking her to choose between red and black on a couple of occasions. It seemed apparent that she had done this sort of thing before. A few times she won, more often she lost. By Tracy's rough reckoning she was at one point about even when Tracy felt a kick on her leg under the table. She had never been a gambler and well knew that on games like this the odds were always in favour of the house, unless someone was very lucky and also had the willpower to stop, it was a sure way to lose money. The whole thing seemed hugely out of character and she wondered – again – what on Earth Mary was up to. Nevertheless, given the agreed signal, she reached into her handbag and pressed the Call button. A second or two later Mary's phone rang, the sound clear above the babble of noise around them.

Mary turned away from the table and reached into her handbag to extract her phone and answered it. Only one side of the conversation was audible, and of course Tracy knew there was no other side, but what Mary said was heard by everyone at the table.

"Hello... yes, it's me....What? Oh no... How bad?... Right, I'll come, of course I'll come, which hospital?... Okay, Right I'm on my way. Bye" Mary then turned to the croupier, a Mediterranean type who despite being immaculately dressed looked as slippery as a buttered ice rink. She offered him an apology and said she had to leave, explaining that it was an emergency and that there had been an accident. They left the table and Mary returned to the counter with her remaining chips, a quantity much the same as the amount she had been given earlier on their arrival. Tracy hovered nearby during the transaction that ensued and then followed at Mary's heels as she walked out and onto the street.

"Now, please, please tell me what's going on. What was all this about? And is someone really in hospital? No. Ridiculous. There can't be, can there?" Mary offered no answer, stepped to the kerb and flagged down a cab giving the driver her home address. Once they were sitting inside she finally spoke.

"Okay, now I'll explain," Mary smiled, "but I wanted it to be a surprise. First, the casino: you should know that I am not a gambler, I know it's a mugs game, if you are ever tempted, resist. That said I suspect it won't surprise you to hear that amongst what I am left with from Marty is, well, let's just say there's a good deal of cash. And cash is all very well but I need to have money in the bank so that I can pay bills, use a credit card and so on. And these days if you start paying large amounts of cash into your bank account then it will doubtless prompt some very intrusive questions - questions I don't want to answer. Right?" Mary paused for a moment and Tracy nodded, it being clear that no more than a nod was going to be allowed.

"So, I brought some money here and used it to buy chips, I made out I was a proper player and then, after just a few minutes play, I contrived to stop – to rush to a hospital – and did so while my pot was much the same as at the start. Then, when I went back to the counter, I got them to pay the money due me into my bank account. They'll do that, well most such places will do that, after all punters don't want to walk out of such an establishment with great bundles of cash - it wouldn't be safe now would it? You know what the West End's like these days. All clear now?"

"Yes, well, I guess so, but I'm not sure why you brought me along, your finances are none of my business, especially... well, especially some of them." Tracy stopped, uncertain what to say next; it still all still seemed rather mysterious.

"I brought you because you need to know about such things. There are a variety of ways of dealing with, let's call it special cash, and I can explain how..." This time Tracy did interrupt.

"But I don't have the sort of money that would need me to..." It was Mary's turn to interrupt, but she was interrupted in turn as the taxi stopped outside her door and their conversation was put on hold. They both clambered out, Mary paid the driver and invited Tracy into the house for a drink. As usual she would not go further until the drinks were ready and on the table.

"Right, you will understand, I felt this bit was best said in private, the connecting window was closed in the cab but even so... anyway, first of all, and I want no argument about this, not a word, not a single word, you must promise." Mary paused and looked at Tracy in a way that forbade any resistance; Tracy found she had no idea where this was going on or what she should say. She certainly had no clue what was coming next and remained silent. There was a brief pause while Mary looked expectant then she continued, the promise assumed to have been made.

"The money in the safe at the lock up, you know what Marty stole from that awful Godwin man, it's more than I need; Marty left me very well provided for – I want you to have it and

I believe that's an arrangement of which Marty would approve." There was silence as she stopped speaking and Tracy, frozen in shock, said nothing.

"Your face is a picture, my dear!" Mary burst out laughing, and Tracy found she had no idea what to say. It flashed through her mind that deciding to respond to Marty's 'Apprentice wanted' notice was the best thing she had done after several years of bad decisions at school and in dead end jobs. Getting the job with Marty and finding she liked it enough to pull herself together had set her on a path leading in a very different and very satisfactory direction. Now, well... all this was extraordinary, and she still didn't know what to say.

At last, she found her tongue, a brief attempt at arguing was scotched by Mary within a few words, so she voiced her thanks as best she could all the while thinking that whatever she said was a million miles from what was appropriate and necessary. It was a while before, still in shock, she set off for home by which time she found she had drunk a little too much of the celebratory drink Mary had insisted was essential to the moment.

A few days later Tracy and Jim took Mary for a slap-up dinner at what they had discovered was her favourite restaurant, Fredericks in Camden Passage. It had taken a good deal of protracted persuasion to get Mary to accept that such a gesture was necessary and, while Tracy thought it was wholly inadequate in every way, the fact that Mary had finally agreed did make her feel just a little better.

Epilogue:

Three months later...

Only one loose end

As Tracy and Jim sat in the living area of their new abode, a small flat on the north side of the borough, a very small flat truth be told as they had been disposed to be careful despite Tracy's recent good fortune, they reflected on the time since they had met.

"I still can't believe it," said Tracy, "our own place! And, just think, about eighteen months ago I was living with my Mum, arguing with her every time our paths crossed, and battling with cardboard boxes on a daily basis. Small this place may be but it's great and I'm pleased it's ours, together I mean, well, as long as we keep up the mortgage payments! It's all been rather quick though, hasn't it... you and me that is." Jim, sitting alongside her on the sofa, put an arm round her before replying.

"I've got no complaints, and I sometimes think if it wasn't for all that business with Marty I might never have plucked up the courage to come into the shop and speak to you. Funny how things work out isn't it?"

"I guess so," said Tracy. "One minute we didn't even know each other and now here we are living together and with you doing some work in the shop." As Tracy had continued to run the shop and continued also to expand the range of what she did by working with Marty's friend Steve a few times a month, she had also decided that the shop could not be best run solo. She had to have some sort of help. Meanwhile Jim had decided a trade might be no bad thing for him. He still had his stall in the market, and he had help with running that, but he had started to work some days at the locksmith's as well. Tracy had taken on Marty's mantel as mentor and tutor and thought Jim was making good progress. They not only had the flat but had their own business too.

Importantly, no more had been heard from the police. They imagined they must have written off the incident with George Godwin following Marty's death, from their perspective it must have seemed that it was a case of accepting that they would in fact never know the detail of what happened on the night Godwin died, after all both the people present were now dead. However this was in all probability compensated for by the fact that Godwin himself could no longer get up to any more trouble. The pair were pleased to have done Rhona McDonald a favour, and allowed Mary to exercise Marty's code as well; they still looked at the website once in a while and recent visits showed that Bunting Hall was running properly again. Mary was doing pretty well without Marty. She had her moments, of course, and her life was different now as she filled the time they had spent together in other ways. She now did regular shifts at the nearby Headway charity shop, this being the main charity focussing on stroke victims in terms of both care and research, and she had also donated a good many of Marty's clothes and the like to them to help raise funds. She called in to see them at the shop now and then and sometimes met them at the café.

"Mary seems to be coping well these days," said Tracy. "I always thought of her as a quiet one, always there for Marty, but rather old fashioned and set in her ways. Then my impression of her began to change, first when Marty was sick, she stood no nonsense with Constable Short. Then when we found the jewels, she became relentless in her desire to get them back to their rightful owner.

Then she not only refused to take no for an answer about Godwin's money, but it turned out she knew all about how to put such cash to use without prompting awkward questions."

"I suppose so, it's the quiet ones who sometimes surprise you it's said," said Jim, who was still feeling overwhelmed by Mary's decision regarding the money, and it had not least left them both wondering about just how 'comfortable', as she had put it, Marty had left her and what unknown adventures he had undertaken to create that situation. He was quite the rogue they had decided but deserved the old phrase 'lovable rogue' and had had many good qualities.

"Do you know what Mary told me the other day?" Tracy asked and Jim shook his head. "Turns out that the Godwin job was one Marty had done on his own, he overheard about the man moving to Portugal in a pub and checked it all out himself. He and Mary never talked about what happened on the day, as it were, with his little expeditions. That had always been a firm rule – if questions were ever asked there would never be anything Mary could say. Sensible enough, I guess. But sometimes, most other times in fact, it was Mary that suggested and researched who he would go after. She not only had a regular role, she was an important part of his second business. How about that? Who'd have thought it, eh? I think that given what I learnt about them through what happened to Marty she feels I may as well know it all now. And you will never believe this, she also told me that if I ever felt I wanted to follow in Marty's footsteps she would be pleased to give me a hand! She even said she had an ideal someone in mind to start me off."

"What? I can't believe it, talk about being a dark horse. Whatever did you say to that?" Tracy said nothing for a moment, smiled, looked serious and then smiled again.

"I said I'd think about it," she said.

END

Acknowledgements

I have had a large number of books published, more non-fiction than fiction, though my last three books to be published have been novels. With all of it, like every writer, I am very aware that writing is essentially a solitary activity. Where from and how ideas appear is largely a mystery to most writers of fiction. However, certainly what writers call the BOSHOK stage – Bum on Seat, Hands on Keyboard is necessarily solitary, it is a prescribed and slog made satisfying when you feel something worthwhile is resulting.

However, writing, like so much else, is fuelled by contact with other people and, for me, those that assist come in two main varieties.

First, other writers: I enjoy the company of other writers and belong to various writing groups including the Brentwood Writers' Circle, a body of some fifty members of which, for some three years, I was Chairman. I am also one of the few male associate members of the national Society of Woman Writers and Journalists (in fact I was recently elected a Fellow) and a member of the Society of Authors. People from all of these, people in small writing groups too as well as individual writers with whom I have had contact over the years have all helped my writing generally, and this book in particular, both motivationally and technically.

Secondly, friends, relations and contacts who may not write themselves, but encourage me in what I do whilst also making regular attempts to distract me away from my computer (though I wouldn't have that any other way!). Thinking of both groups there is a temptation to write a long list of names. I will resist that and mention just two: Jacqueline Connelly, always my first reader and a reliable mistake spotter and comment giver, and Lloyd Bonson, publisher extraordinaire, who again did a splendid job turning my manuscript into a finished book.

To everyone, whether you helped directly or indirectly, and in whatever way, I offer my sincere thanks. Especially if you have bought one of my books!

About the Author

Patrick Forsyth is a much-published author best known for many non-fiction books. Many of those offer guidance to people working in organisations, for example *Successful Time Management* (Kogan Page) is a bestselling title on its subject and is now in its sixth edition. He has also had three light-hearted books of travel writing published: *First class at last!*, *Beguiling Burma* and *Smile because it happened*. All are set in South East Asia.

Another, rather different, title is the book *Empty when half full*, a hilarious critique of miscommunication so bad that it misleads and amuses. He has had three novels published previously: *Long Overdue*, a light mystery concerning a missing person, *Loose Ends* is (loosely) a sequel, and the third is *A Rather Curious Crime*. He is active in the writing world, writing regularly for *Writing Magazine*, giving talks and running writing workshops; he also has involvements with several writing groups large and small. He lives in Maldon in north Essex and writes looking out on the estuary of the River Blackwater; this is his fourth novel.

Also from the Author

First Class At Last!
An Antidote to Past Travel Horrors
More Than 1,200 Miles in Extreme Luxury

Fed up with the strenuous process of travel: the slow queues, the delays, the crowds and the extreme discomfort of the average economy airline seat?

Patrick Forsyth decided it was time to do something about this. He arranged a trip designed to be the antidote to the routine travel misery - and booked a trip travelling only first class.

The first challenge was to decide where to go. He decided to fly to Bangkok, stay in the world renowned Oriental Hotel, continue onto Singapore and stay at the equally famous Raffles Hotel. He then travelled in style back to Bangkok on the Eastern and Orient Express, where he spent two nights on what many people regard as the best train ride in the world, and finally concluded his travel at a luxury spa on the beach, to recover.

Along the way, the author meets a rock and roll musician; visits dubious bars and colourful markets; has an encounter with the bodyguards of the Thai Royal Family; and embarks on a boat trip along the River Kwai. This lively, amusing account of luxury travel, highlights what every traveller secretly longs to do - travel in style and grandeur.

"…witty and full of facts …" **Essex Life**

"… Lively, witty and wry." **Select Books**

"… it reminded me of Bryson…"
Neal Asher, bestselling author of Gridlinked

Long Overdue

By his own admission, Philip is living a humdrum life in the Essex coastal town of Maldon.

His new boss at the town library is a pain in the neck, making even the job he loves difficult, and he longs for something to kick start him out of what he admits is a bit of a rut. Soon after a new and unexpected friendship begins he determines to make some changes.

Then one day his routine walk to work has him finding a dead body, involved with the police and feeling he must help his new friend by investigating a mystery from years past.

As events following the death carry him along, an abandoned sailing boat, half a letter and a surprising alliance sees him seeking to unravel the mystery of a missing person.

He quickly realises that dialling the emergency services that spring morning is leading to changes that will affect his life, his job and his future as well as having him travel abroad and make some surprisingly impulsive decisions

"Patrick Forsyth has written many non-fiction books but this is his first novel. It comes with a real ear for dialogue and a pulse-quickening sense of risk. As for Philip, he is a thoroughly well-rounded protagonist for whom you root from the start."
The Good Book Guide